GO AHEAD!

"Where are you going, Molly?" Laura called out.

"Home!" Molly answered without turning around.

"Which is where? Kansas?" Stevie yelled at Molly's back as kids stood around watching the girls fight.

Molly whipped off her mittens and hat that were making her itchy. "It's better than here!" she yelled back.

"Well, just go ahead!" Stevie shouted, while Meg and Laura looked on in horror at the sound of those terrible words.

P.S. We'll Miss You
Yours 'Til the Meatball Bounces
2 Sweet 2 B 4-Gotten
Remember Me, When This You See
Sealed with a Hug

SEALED WITH A HUG

Deirdre Corey

AN
APPLE
PAPERBACK

SCHOLASTIC INC.
New York Toronto London Auckland Sydney

ISBN 0-590-44027-6

Copyright © 1990 by Fastback Press. All rights reserved. Published by Scholastic Inc. APPLE PAPERBACKS is a registered trademark of Scholastic Inc. FRIENDS 4-EVER is a trademark of Scholastic Inc.

12 11 10 9 8 7 6 5 4 3 2 1   0 1 2 3 4 5/9
                Printed in the U.S.A.   40
        First Scholastic printing, October 1990

To Melissa Golab

THE FRIENDSHIP PIE

Molly Quindlen counted the dishes. One chipped mixing bowl, a cut-glass pickle dish, a small silver tray, and the platter with the painted turkey were all she had left to dry. In just a few minutes she could try calling her best friends, Stevie Ames, Laura Ryder, and Meg Milano in Rhode Island again, and she could hardly wait.

"They must be home by now," she said out loud to the china gravy boat still in her hand. She had already dialed Stevie's number four times in the last couple of hours, but no one had answered. Same thing at Laura's and at Meg's. Where were they, anyway? It upset her to think that her old friends were off doing things she didn't know about.

Molly walked slowly to the cool pantry just off the kitchen in her grandpa's old farmhouse. She gave the little gravy boat one last wipe with the dish towel and set it down — a bit roughly — on the shelf where it belonged. Darn. Her Thanksgiving in Kansas had been perfect, from a brisk morning horseback ride on Chocolate to the success of her pumpkin pie. But what fun was it when there was nobody to tell?

Molly heard the oak clock strike eight and reminded herself it was only nine o'clock back in Camden, Rhode Island where she *really* lived. There was still plenty of time to call her friends before her perfect day was over. She tiptoed to the hall just outside the kitchen and picked up the receiver.

"Four-oh-one," she whispered to herself as she dialed the Rhode Island area code again. Stevie's phone rang twelve-and-a-half times before Molly gave up. After ten rings, she knew what she didn't want to know — Meg wasn't home yet, either. Just as she was about to dial Laura's number, Mrs. Quindlen walked into the hallway.

"Aw, Molly, you're just making yourself miserable," her mother said gently. "Why don't

2

you wait awhile since you just tried calling a few minutes ago?"

"I did not!" Molly protested, though the receiver was still warm in her hand.

"Maybe they're at Mrs. Plumley's or the Barbellas'," Mrs. Quindlen suggested.

"Do you think so, Mom?" Molly could handle that. Maybe her three friends weren't off having fun without her instead of being at home to get her call. Maybe their parents were dragging them around on holiday visits to elderly people in the neighborhood. Molly knew all about *those*, where the girls had to remember their pleases and thank-yous and not knock over Mrs. Plumley's china bulldogs. She smiled, just thinking of her best friend, Stevie, trying to sit still while Mrs. Ames and Mrs. Plumley discussed the best way to make gravy.

"That's where they are, I bet," Molly said. "Hey, maybe I can — "

"Now don't go getting any ideas about calling the Barbellas or Mrs. Plumley," Mrs. Quindlen, the mind reader, began before Molly finished. "We agreed, Molly. Three long distance calls. Short ones. You can't go calling around the whole neighborhood to track down the girls. I mean it."

"All right, all right," Molly groaned. But she

couldn't wait to talk to the friends she had left a year before when she and her family had moved to Kansas. They were only supposed to have stayed a year to help Mr. Quindlen's ailing father in his store, but time had gone on.

Mrs. Quindlen peeked into the kitchen. "You were such a help today, Molly," she sighed. "Thanks so much. Why don't you just finish up, then try your calls a little later, okay?"

"Oh, fine," Molly muttered.

The kitchen was still warm from the day's cooking but not the kind of cozy-warm Molly had liked earlier in the day. Now she felt tired and full from too many kinds of foods. The ties on her red corduroy jumper dangled nearly to the floor. Her white tights had gone a bit gray during an hour of living room soccer with her six-year-old brother, Scotty, after dinner, and her patent leather slip-ons looked dull and scuffy now.

Molly dried the small silver tray, then breathed on it to make it shine. "Ugh," she said. She stuck out her tongue at the girl who stared back from the bottom of the tray. Her cheeks looked beet red, and she could see that the big bow she had spent *hours* placing in her chin-length brown hair had slipped halfway down the side of her head. Her fine, straight hair never could be held in place for long by any bow or hairband. When she grew tired of her getting-crabby face, she slid the silver tray onto a pantry shelf and then finished in the kitchen.

"I'm going upstairs," she yelled to the rest of the family in the living room when she was done.

"Good pie today, Molly," Mr. Quindlen called back without looking away from the football game he was watching.

Scotty was too busy chasing around his own small football to notice Molly, and Mrs. Quindlen was settled in a chair with the morning newspaper she hadn't had a chance to look at all day.

" 'Night, Grandpa," Molly said, but Grandpa Quindlen was sleeping through the third quarter while the Quindlens' dog, Riggs, snored softly by his side, probably dreaming of prairie dogs.

"Here, boy," Molly called to Riggs, but only his ears and tail moved. Then Molly held out a piece of turkey she had smuggled out of the refrigerator for just this purpose, and Riggs sprang across the living room.

"That better not be table food," Mr. Quindlen warned, still glued to the television.

"It's Thanksgiving for dogs, too, Dad!" Molly said for about the sixth time that day.

Before they could get into *that* discussion

again, Mr. Quindlen yelled, "Touchdown!" and Molly was saved from a lecture about dog nutrition.

"C'mon, Riggs," Molly whispered. She thought about how nice and warm her feet would feel when Riggs was sleeping on them.

I'll just take my time, Molly told herself on the way to her room. Then they're sure to be home.

The little upstairs bedroom in her grandfather's house was always chilly on the nights when only the downstairs fireplace was lit. "Brr." Molly wriggled as fast as she could into her flannel pajamas and slipper-socks.

"Good boy, Riggs. You make a nice warm spot for me." Molly slid under the pile of blankets she used on cold nights like this one. Riggs tilted his head for a bit of ear rubbing, then curled himself up again for yet another nap.

The oak clock downstairs chimed once. Eight-thirty Kansas, nine-thirty Rhode Island. Stevie, Meg, and Laura just *had* to be home by now, didn't they? Molly pulled her phone over to the bed.

"We are s-o-o-o jealous," she remembered Meg exclaiming way back when Molly first got the phone. They thought Molly's phone was just the thing for important calls to the Time-of-Day and Weatherphone numbers.

"It's only because we're moving to Kansas," she had explained to Stevie, Meg, and Laura back then.

The phone still seemed brand-new to Molly. She was much more used to writing to her old friends through the club Meg had organized just before Molly moved away. Out of all the clubs they had ever had, Friends 4-Ever was the best.

"It should be called Friends 4-Never," Molly grumbled now. She looked at the three separate stacks of letters on her desk. Today she needed more than letters. She needed to *hear* her friends' voices, just to make sure they were still thinking about her and waiting for the day when she would come home for good.

Whenever that was.

After tapping out all three phone numbers with no luck, Molly flopped back onto her stack of pillows.

There was a soft knock at the door. "Come in."

"Are they back yet?" her mother asked. She sat down by Riggs at the far end of the bed.

"No!" Molly said as though her mother were personally responsible for what her friends were doing in Rhode Island.

"Well, you still have time. Don't let it spoil your day, Molly." Her mother picked up Molly's letter-writing clipboard and put it on the bed. "Maybe you could start a letter now and try calling later on," her mother suggested. "I noticed you got two letters this week."

"Yeah, and you know what Meg said? 'Happy Thanksgiving. I'll write a longer letter next week.' She wrote that in her last two letters!" Molly sniffled. "Only without the 'Happy Thanksgiving' part." With that, Molly slid all the way down under the blankets until she disappeared.

"Well, Stevie's last envelope looked pretty fat," Mrs. Quindlen said to the angry lump on the bed.

A muffled voice spoke back. "It was just the sports page from the *Camden News* with her soccer team's record! They hardly ever write me any *real* letters anymore. They're forgetting all about me."

"Well, maybe if you write a nice long letter about today, they'll get the idea to write back a little longer next time," Mrs. Quindlen suggested. "Remember what you said when you were making your pie yesterday?"

Molly wriggled her head out of the blankets so her mother would get a good view of her furious face. "You mean about my pumpkin pie being like the Friends 4-Ever? Well, I was wrong. Mud pie is more like it!"

Mrs. Quindlen tried not to smile. "Now, Molly. Just yesterday you told me Laura was the sugar, Stevie was the spice, and Meg was the — "

"Rotten eggs," Molly cut in.

"Oh, honey, they're just out, that's all. Maybe they tried to call *you* when we were out on our walk today."

"They did not, and who cares, anyway?" Molly flattened a pillow around her ears. "I'm never going to see them again, never! I'm stuck in Kansas forever."

"Not forever, Molly. Grandpa's much better. He's working longer hours at the hardware store. If everything keeps going the way it is now, we'll be moving back for good next summer."

"Next summer's a million years away!" Molly cried, and right at that moment it was. "The other night I had a dream about my room on Half Moon Lane, and when I woke up I couldn't remember if the little houses on my wallpaper were red or pink."

"Pink," Mrs. Quindlen said softly. "And they'll still be pink when we get back."

"When I'm seventy-two, you mean?" Molly said. She jutted out her chin as far as she could. "I didn't ask to move out here. You and Dad made me. I just want to go home and see my friends again!"

"I know, Molly, but these things take time," Mrs. Quindlen said on her way out. "I promise something will happen very soon. We'll talk about it tomorrow when you're not so tired."

After Mrs. Quindlen left the room, Molly sniffled and sniffled. She bent over Riggs and snuggled close. His fur was warm and soft and just what she needed.

"You're a good boy, Riggsy," she kept saying to him. "Remember when I found you after you ran away 'cause you didn't want to come to Kansas?"

Riggs sighed at that very moment.

"You do remember, don't you, boy?"

Of course, Molly couldn't deny that Riggs was a Kansas dog now and liked nothing better than to run free and chase the country critters who hid out in the dried cornstalks. Just that morning he had stood guard at two new gopher holes out in the back field while Molly gave the Pollards' horse Chocolate a good run around her grandfather's property. Like Riggs, there was a little bit of Kansas in Molly, too.

Molly spied her clipboard on the bed just where her mother had left it. Maybe she would write her friends a letter. Even if they didn't deserve one.

She set the phone back on the end of her dresser and grabbed her clipboard and rainbow pencil.

Dear Stevie, Meg, and Laura,

In case you're wondering why I'm writing to all three of you, it's because I have a long letter to write, not just "Hi" (like some people I know).

I've been trying to call you for over two hours, but you're probably at Mrs. Plumley's talking about what grade you're in now and how tall you're getting. Boring, boring!

I wasn't going to tell you this 'cause I was mad about you not being at home when I needed to talk to you, but my mom says I shouldn't wreck my whole holiday.

The main reason I'm writing is to tell you about Chocolate (again) and how Kristy Pollard let me exercise him this morning since the Pollards went to Wichita for Thanksgiving. Even though I missed watching the Thanksgiving Parade with you guys, it was fun riding a horse instead. (My mom sent me to the Rainbow Dairy Ranch to get real sage for our turkey. Sort of like Little House on the Prairie, except my dad watched football practically all day!)

The sage in the turkey was good, but what was better was my Friends 4-Ever pumpkin pie. Last month I won second prize for it in the Future Farmers booth at the Cross Plains Grange. And even though we couldn't be together today you were in my pie!

The pie would taste like plain old mush if it were just pumpkin and eggs. What made it the best (okay, second best) is sugar (Laura), ginger (Stevie, of course, with one or two prickly cloves), and cinnamon (Meg). I guess that makes me the crust ('cause I'm so flaky). I don't think I'm ever going to be a Future Farmer (I hope not, anyway), but making my pie and sharing it with everybody today made me think of you (even if your latest letters have been kind of short. No more sports clippings, Stevie, okay???).

Please write me a long letter about

12

*Thanksgiving in Crispin Landing. If you
don't, my next recipe is going to be Friends
4-Ever sour pickles. I mean it!!!!!!!*

Your Friend 4-Ever,

Molly

Molly had no sooner dotted her last exclamation point than the phone rang. "Hello, Molly speaking," she answered.

"Hello, we're taking a survey of birds in Kansas," a voice said. "Could you tell me what you get when you put two ducks in a crate?"

"Hold on. I'll get my mom," Molly answered, puzzled.

"A box of quackers! Ha! Ha! Ha!"

"Stevie Ames? Is that you?" Molly shrieked.

"And Meg," another voice broke in.

"And Laura. I'm on the kitchen extension at Stevie's! Happy Thanksgiving! Even though it's practically over."

"You guys! I tried to call you a million times today. I thought you went to another planet or something," Molly said breathlessly. "So where were you all this time, anyway?"

"Visiting Mrs. Hansen. It was neat being in your house again," Stevie told her. "She let us sort out her recipe box and stuff while the grown-ups talked about world events and whether this year is colder than last year. We had fun."

"You did?" Molly said, feeling a small pang of jealousy.

"What's the matter, Molly?" Even two thousand miles away, Laura noticed how quiet Molly got at the mention of Mrs. Hansen's name.

"I . . . I just wish you didn't like Mrs. Hansen s-o-o-o much. Since she's living in my house and all. You sure do go there a lot."

"She made your mom's popcorn balls for Halloween," Stevie said, trying to defend the nice elderly lady who was renting the Quindlens' house while they were gone. "She wants to meet you."

"Well, I don't want . . . never mind." Molly had to swallow twice to make all her mixed-up feelings go away. She changed the subject from Mrs. Hansen to something they could all talk about without getting upset. Food. "So what'd you have for Thanksgiving?"

"Turkey, of course," Meg said. "With cornbread dressing."

"Yucky turnips," Stevie added. "Blech!"

"Yummy yams," Laura chimed in. "With marshmallows on top."

After listening to their long recitation of all the menus, Molly felt better. "Bet you didn't have Friends 4-Ever Pie," she teased.

Stevie, Meg, and Laura all screamed out, "What's that?"

"You'll find out," Molly said mysteriously. "When you get my next letter. I almost finished it when the phone rang. And by the way, while you're waiting for it, some of you — I won't say who — promised longer letters soon."

There was a lot of quiet on the Rhode Island end of the phone.

"We'll have an emergency letter-writing meeting tonight," Meg pledged. "During our sleepover or before we go to the mall tomorrow to start our Christmas shopping."

"O-o-o lucky." Molly felt another quick pang. A feeling-left-out kind of pang this time.

"We're shopping for your presents first." Laura always knew what to say to make her faraway friend feel a little closer.

"All I really want are some long letters, okay?" Molly said. "Fat ones."

"My clipboard's right here under my soccer shoes," Stevie said.

"We'll all write to you, Molly," Meg added. "Right away."

"Okay," Molly said. "I'm really glad you guys called. I was starting to feel like you forgot all about me being in Kansas."

"Never!" the girls shouted into the phone.

"My mom's making weird faces and hand signals," Stevie broke in. "I think that means we have to get off. So watch out for tornadoes, okay?"

"And don't forget to finish your letter," Meg added.

"I won't. But first I'm going back for seconds," Molly said.

"Seconds of what?" Laura wanted to know.

"Friends 4-Ever Pie. What else?"

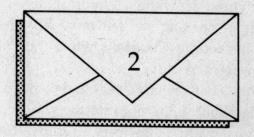

THE GOOD-BYE TREE

"No slug-a-beds in Kansas," Molly mumbled when she heard the awful buzz of her alarm go off at six-thirty the day after Thanksgiving. This was a thought she often had when she had to get up early, even on weekends and vacations. She could tell by the milky light coming from the window that it was going to be a *Wizard-of-Oz* kind of day — the sky big and gray just like the black-and-white part of her favorite movie.

It has taken a long time to get used to waking up so early in Kansas, but Molly learned quickly that if she wanted to ride a horse, she had to feed a horse. That meant helping out at the Pollard farm where Chocolate, her favorite horse, lived. Kristy Pollard, Molly's closest Kansas friend, had taught her how to ride when the Quindlens first came to Kansas. Now, in exchange for stable chores, Molly could ride Chocolate anytime she wanted. Unfortunately, on this cold, gray morning she felt more like sleeping late than feeding Chocolate while the Pollards were away in Wichita.

Chores. That's what Kansas had plenty of. Just thinking about going out into the windy day to do chores made Molly very grumpy. Back in Rhode Island, Stevie, Laura, and Meg were sound asleep in their sleeping bags and wouldn't have to get up for hours, Molly thought. Then it was off to the mall in Providence to get a jump on their urgent Christmas shopping. All that seemed so far away.

"You up, Molly?" Mr. Quindlen called out from the bathroom.

Molly stuck out one arm. "Yup." Next came the other arm, then one leg, followed by the other.

When Molly reached for her boots under the bed she saw her clipboard. Her Friends 4-Ever letter was all ready to mail. Or was it? Maybe she would just wait and see if her friends *really* were going to write the long letters they promised last night.

To stay warm as long as possible, Molly pulled up her riding jeans over her pajama bottoms and stretched herself into her thick gray sweatshirt, pajama top and all. She tucked in everything so her mother wouldn't find out about her latest keeping-warm trick.

"Molly, it's a quarter to seven!" Mrs. Quindlen called up the stairs.

"I'm coming, I'm coming!" Molly yelled back none-too-sweetly. What was the big rush, anyway? She pulled on her boots and clomped downstairs.

"Hey, it's about time, sleepyhead," Mr. Quindlen told Molly when she came into the bright, warm kitchen.

" 'Morning, Molly Melinda," Grandpa said the way he did every morning. Molly usually liked being reminded that she not only had her grandmother's heart-shaped face but her pretty name, too. Today, though, she was too tired to give her grandfather a big smile to go with her "Good morning."

"Long phone call last night?" Mrs. Quindlen asked as she shook cereal into Molly's bowl.

"Three phone calls in one," Molly answered. "Meg and Laura were on the extensions at Stevie's."

"Good way to save on phone bills, four people

19

talking at once," Mr. Quindlen said with a smile. "What're the three Friends 4-Ever cooking up now?"

"A trip to Providence to start on Christmas shopping. Like we used to always do the day after Thanksgiving." Molly paused to give her parents plenty of time to feel sorry for her. "Could we drive to Wichita today?" Molly said next. "To the mall? After I do my chores at the Pollards', I mean?"

Scotty looked up from his cereal bowl. "I'm workin' at the store today. Grandpa said I could. Puttin' out the shovels and the plastic Santas."

"We never get to do anything," Molly complained.

"Now, Molly, the day after Thanksgiving is one of the biggest days at the hardware store. We're not shoppers anymore, we're the ones who get things ready for the shoppers," Mr. Quindlen reminded Molly. "Besides, I thought you had big plans for setting up the Christmas display in the store window this afternoon."

"I guess."

"You usually like taking charge of my store, Molly Melinda." Grandpa Quindlen looked a little hurt. "Why, you do just as good a job with that window as your grandma did. 'Course last year it looked like the North Pole and not a place where folks could get a hammer or a wrench, but we did a pretty good holiday business, thanks to you."

Molly bit her lip. She *loved* doing important jobs at Quindlen's Hardware and helping Grandpa keep the store running. She just wished Meg hadn't been so full of plans about what everyone in Rhode Island would be doing today.

"Sorry, Grandpa," Molly said. "I'll be there at noon. Just like I promised."

Molly was glad she'd smoothed things over with her grandfather. It wasn't his fault she was so touchy this morning.

"Hope Grandpa can do without you at Christmas, Molly," Mr. Quindlen suddenly announced. He had a big smile on his face and his hands behind his back.

"Yeah, 'cause we're goin' to — "

"Scotty! Shh," Mrs. Quindlen whispered, putting a finger to her lips.

"Here." Mr. Quindlen handed Molly a small box wrapped in Santa paper. "It's an early Christmas present."

Molly didn't quite know what to do with the box.

"Go ahead, open it," Mrs. Quindlen urged.

Molly carefully removed the wrapping paper and lifted the lid. Lying inside was a piece of paper marked *Airline Ticket — Round Trip — Kansas/Rhode Island*. In each of the corners were some smudges that looked a little like airplanes.

"I made those," Scotty chimed in. He leaned in toward his big sister and pointed to his drawings.

Molly's heart pounded. Did this mean she was going to Rhode Island?

Mrs. Quindlen smiled. "We're all going to Rhode Island. For the whole Christmas vacation."

Molly's brain was whirling with questions. "Where are we going to stay? What about Grandpa's store? When will — ?"

"Whoa! Rewind, rewind," Mr. Quindlen broke in. "Mrs. Hansen's spending a few weeks with her son and then with her daughter in Camden so she won't be alone for Christmas. She sent us a note with her December rent."

"That's what gave us the big idea, Molly," Mrs. Quindlen continued. "We can stay in our old house. It won't be quite the same, of course, with Mrs. Hansen's things there for now, but — "

"But my room will still be there!" Molly cried with joy.

"We ordered the airline tickets just a couple of days ago and decided to surprise you," Mrs.

Quindlen said. "I got Scotty to draw you a pretend ticket until the real ones come."

Molly grabbed Scotty and tickled his neck and his stomach until he screamed for mercy. "You kept a secret for two whole days!" Molly cried. She ruffled his fine brown hair. "You monster!"

"Brian Pollard's going to do some of the heavy work at the store," Grandpa Quindlen told Molly. " 'Course he won't be so good at arranging birdhouses and teapots in the windows. Not like you, but maybe I can get a shovel or two on display for a change!"

"Yippee!" Molly cried. She danced circles around the kitchen table and popped dry Cheerios into her mouth one at a time. "I can't wait to call Stevie, Laura, and Meg. Can I?" Molly skidded to a stop. "No, I know. I'm going to tell them at the end of my letter. Wait 'til they read *that* out loud at the next Friends 4-Ever meeting!"

"We'll hear the cheers clear to Kansas," Mr. Quindlen predicted.

Molly flew out of the kitchen and took the stairs two at a time, making as much noise as Chocolate would have if he were allowed to gallop upstairs. Molly heard somebody call out something about not finishing breakfast, but she was too excited to think about anything as ordinary as food when something so super-duper

23

extraordinary was only a few weeks away.

She was going home!

Molly grabbed her clipboard and pencil and scribbled as fast as she could.

P.S. I just got the biggest, best Christmas present ever, a visit to my best, best friends. I'm coming home! C U soon.

Your Friend 4-Ever,

Molly

Molly folded the sheets of her letter so fast the folds were all crooked, and the thick wad of rainbow paper barely fit into the envelope. She pulled a long strip of tape and pressed it down on the flap so the whole thing wouldn't burst. Rummaging through the 'N' Stuff box where she kept tiny treasures like old pebbles, movie stubs, and even a piece of pavement from Half Moon Lane in Rhode Island, Molly found just what she was looking for. She tore off a teddy bear from a strip of holiday stickers the Friends 4-Ever had given her the year before. Across the teddy's Santa hat was the message: "Have a *beary* merry Christmas." Molly positioned it on the

24

point of the flap where her friends would see it right away.

"There," she said, finally satisfied with the job.

In a flash, Molly was downstairs again to bundle up for the cold day.

"We'll drop you at the Pollards' when we drive to the store," her father said on his way out to start the van.

"Sure, Dad. It looks freeeeezing out."

"Well, I'll warm up the car so it won't be too bad."

In a few minutes the only van in Cross Plains with Rhode Island license plates bumped along the back dirt road. Molly pressed her nose against the glass and watched as the Pollards' silo and farm buildings seemed to grow out of the horizon.

"You won't forget my letter, will you, Dad?" Molly asked when they pulled up in front of the Pollards' place.

"How can I when I can hardly stand up carrying it?" He patted his bulging jacket pocket where he had safely put the letter. "What's in here, anyway? The Sunday edition of the *Wichita Eagle*?"

"It's an important letter, Dad!" Molly said firmly. "So make sure you drop it right at the post office. Before you open the hardware store, even. Promise?"

"We'll see that he does, Molly." Grandpa Quindlen slid open the van door so Molly could get out. "Now don't go forgetting our lunch at Annie's Cafe. It's pot roast day, you know, with those mashed potatoes you like."

"I won't forget, Grandpa," Molly yelled, but her words were lost in the blast of air that unwound her scarf and nearly sent it sailing.

When she reached the old clapboard stable, she was surprised to see the big wooden door flapping back and forth. "I know I locked it yesterday," she said out loud.

"You did," answered a tall girl with a blonde ponytail, when Molly stepped into the warmth of the stable.

"Kristy!" Molly cried out. "I thought you weren't going to be back 'til tomorrow."

Kristy set down the two heavy water pails she was carrying and leaned into a huge pile of hay to keep warm. "We came back from Wichita a day early. My dad couldn't stand being away from the animals another minute," Kristy said with a crooked smile. "Me, neither," she added with a nod toward Starry Night who was chomping on breakfast. "I tried to call you so you

26

wouldn't have to come over, but nobody answered."

"Everybody went to Grandpa's hardware store today. Even Scotty. They have to start putting out the holiday decorations. I'm going there later to help decorate the windows."

Now that Molly's eyes had adjusted to the dim light, she could see that Kristy didn't look as happy to see her as usual. She was stubbing at the dirt floor with the silver tip of her cowboy boot and nervously tugging the end of the red bandana she always tied to the belt loop of her jeans.

Finally she looked directly at Molly. "You'll see my brother, Brian, there this afternoon. Your dad and grandfather are going to train him so he can help out while you're in . . ."

"Rhode Island," Molly finished. "So I guess you know the good news."

"Yeah, I guess I do," Kristy said quietly, slowly rubbing her cheek against Starry Night's glossy black-and-white coat. "Thanks for braiding his tail when you curried Chocolate. My dad said the animals looked like show horses when he came in to check them last night."

"I wanted to surprise you," Molly told her friend.

"You sure did," Kristy said. "Thanks. I just wish I felt the same way about the other surprise."

Molly picked up a pitchfork and dug into the pile of hay the horses needed. As she balanced a huge forkful all the way to Chocolate's stall, she tried to balance the thoughts she was having. Old thoughts about how when somebody goes away, somebody stays behind. Friends 4-Ever had taught her that. That's what the stacks of letters from Stevie, Laura, and Meg were all about.

"Hey, I am glad for you," Kristy said when she noticed Molly's frowning. "But I'm sad for me. I'll miss you. I was hoping you could come to my house on St. Lucia's Day like last year, but your dad told Brian you'll be gone by then."

Visions of a Kansas Christmas swirled around in Molly's head. "Oh," she said, disappointed. "You know I got so excited about going to Rhode Island, I sort of forgot I would be leaving Kansas," Molly confessed. "I'll miss everything."

"Especially the play!"

"Oh, no!" Molly groaned. "That means Tammy's going to get my part."

Every year, Broken Arrow Regional School recreated a prairie Christmas with scenes from one of Molly's favorite *Little House on the Prairie* books. This year Molly was to play the main character, Laura Ingalls Wilder. Kristy had been picked to play Mary Ingalls, the quiet and sweet older sister. With her long blonde hair and sweet face, she was just perfect for the part.

Tammy Larson, on the other hand, was not at all perfect for the part of Laura, but that's just what was going to happen now that Molly was leaving. Tammy had begged and begged Mrs. Brown to be Molly's understudy until the teacher finally gave in. Ever since, Molly and Kristy had the feeling that Tammy secretly wished something would happen to Molly. And something did. She was going to Rhode Island, and now Tammy was going to be the star.

"She's more the Nellie Oleson type," Kristy said, thinking of the snobby character in the *Little House* books. "Uh, I can't believe she's going to play my sister. Sometimes it's hard enough having her as a friend. I sure wish you didn't have to go."

Molly tried hard to think of something to say that would make them both feel better. "I wish I could be in two places at the same time. Here with you, and Chocolate, of course," Molly said, patting the horse's smooth brown coat and giving Kristy a sad sort of smile. "Let's write to each other. I want to hear all about the play and whether Tammy ruins it! We won't miss each other so much if we send letters," Molly said.

"I'd like that," Kristy agreed, nudging her head into Chocolate for comfort. "I'll tell you all about the holiday events so you won't really miss them."

"Thanks. Last year you made our holiday so special. Your whole family did." Molly remembered all the special Swedish holiday customs Kristy and her mother had taught the Quindlens.

"Hey!" Kristy cried, all excited. "It's a little early, but let's do one Christmas thing together now."

"The wheat tree!" Molly cried.

"There it is, over by the tools," Kristy said, pointing to a tall T-shaped pole at the back of the stable. "You get it, and I'll meet you out front after I gather up some wheat stalks from our silo."

Molly separated the wooden pole from the tangle of pitchforks and hoes. What a great idea. She remembered the first time they had decorated the pole with wheat from the Pollards' fields. In the old days, Swedish frontier families set out the pole as a Christmas feast for prairie birds so that there would be a good harvest the following summer. Kristy's mother was half-

Swedish and encouraged her children to keep up some of the old customs.

"Here," Kristy said, handing Molly an armful of golden wheat stalks. "You gather three fat bunches, and we'll attach them to the pole."

Molly pulled together a bouquet of stalks and tapped them on the ground to make sure the stems were even.

Kristy snipped several lengths of fine coppery wire from Mr. Pollard's toolbox. The girls worked silently, tying the wheat bouquets to the pole until it was all filled out and almost looked like a live tree in full bloom.

When they were almost done, Kristy stopped and looked at Molly. "You know what I wish?"

"What?"

"That we not only get a good harvest next year, but that you'll come back to visit every summer."

"But I'm not leaving for good," Molly protested. "I'll be back after vacation. In just a few weeks."

"I wonder," Kristy said, pulling the stalks tight so the wheat would stay on the pole no matter how hard the wind blew. "My brother's been talking about your grandfather's store a lot. He doesn't want to be a full-time farmer just yet.

And . . . you've got to go back to Rhode Island sometime."

Molly didn't dare think about that. She couldn't wait to start her visit, but was she really ready to leave Kansas? Now she wasn't quite so sure.

When the harvest pole was all decorated, the girls set it into the ground by the stable where bobwhites and prairie chickens were sure to find it.

"Merry Christmas, little birds," Kristy said.

"Merry Christmas," Molly repeated. "I'll miss you, Kristy." She looked east across the big Kansas sky to see if any birds were flying in their direction. Her eyes prickled with tears from the icy wind and from the thought that she would be saying good-bye to Kansas very soon.

HOME SWEET HOME

The first familiar thing Molly saw when she woke up was the black clock on the white steeple. She *knew* that clock from somewhere. But where? Molly's eyelids drooped again.

"Hey, Chicken Lickin', wake up," she heard her dad say from the front seat.

When Molly opened her eyes, the white steeple was still there, lit with floodlights that brightened the dark winter night.

Mrs. Quindlen turned around to check on her sleepy children in the backseat. "Know where we are?"

Molly tried to shake the pins-and-needles feelings in her right foot. Her brain was all pins and needles, too, and the darkness of the unfamiliar car made it hard for her to figure out just where she was. "My foot went to sleep."

"Not just your foot. The whole rest of you, too," Mrs. Quindlen said. "You and Scotty have been sleeping since we left the car rental place at the airport in Boston, poor things."

Molly's neck ached when she turned to look at her little brother sound asleep next to her. Scotty was still buckled into his seat belt, and his head slumped on his shoulder.

"Looks like you lost your bet, Molly," Mr. Quindlen said. "Remember, when we got on the plane this morning you said you were going to be awake when we got to Camden?"

Molly's eyes opened wide as something stupendous finally sank in. That familiar clock belonged to the Old Dutch Church in Camden, and the redbrick building next to it was where Molly had once taken ballet. "Is that the Yellow Brick Road, Mom?" she cried, hardly daring to believe that the bright inviting building with the steamed windows was the same coffee shop where she and Stevie, Laura and Meg had eaten dozens of doughnuts dozens of times.

"Hope you still like cinnamon doughnuts, Molly." Mr. Quindlen held up a large white bag in the front seat. "I just ran in and got a dozen of 'em for breakfast tomorrow."

Now Molly understood why a warm cinnamony smell got all jumbled up with the patchwork of thoughts she'd been having as she drifted in and out of sleep during the endless ride from the airport. Cinnamon doughnuts meant the trip was over. She was home now.

"We're here! We're really here!" Molly cried when she finally realized that Camden, Rhode Island, was just outside the car window.

"Now if I can only find the headlights in this jalopy," Mr. Quindlen said as he tried to start the unfamiliar car they had rented. First he turned on the windshield wipers by mistake, then accidentally washed the windshield when he touched something else.

"Daddy, hurry up!" Molly urged. "We're practically there." She wasn't at all sure she could keep herself from running out of the car all the way to her old neighborhood.

"Crispin Landing, here we come, right back where we started from," Mr. Quindlen sang after he finally got the car going.

Molly rubbed her mittened hand across the fogged back window so she could see everything. Camden looked so busy, even at eight-thirty at night. Nothing like Cross Plains, which could sometimes seem like a ghost town when its few shops were closed. A nice ghost town, of course, with friendly ghosts.

Here in Camden there were still people out, buying milk and bread at the 7-Eleven or looking at the menu posted outside Camden's only Mexican restaurant. Casa Miguel was the place where the Friends 4-Ever had started their special collection of cactus-shaped swizzle sticks.

"Drive slowly, Bill, so we can see everything," Molly's mother said softly and with an unmistakable sniffle. "I need to get my bearings."

"Open the floodgates back there. Mom's crying again," Molly's dad announced. But he said it in the same silly way he always did when Mrs. Quindlen cried at the end of sad movies.

"Now, Bill, don't tell me you're not feeling a little bit choked up, too. C'mon," Mrs. Quindlen teased back in between sniffles.

But Mr. Quindlen started singing again. "Open up those golden gates, Crispin Landing, here we come!"

Molly pressed her nose against the cold window so she wouldn't miss a thing, and she didn't. Soon she matched nearly every building with her memories of them. And when Mr. Quindlen turned into Crispin Landing Road where Molly's neighborhood began, she recognized every curve and bump in the road.

"Ooo. There's Laura's," Molly called out. "They have their tree up already. Luckeee. Can we stop?"

"First things first," Mrs. Quindlen said, but it made no difference to Molly. Everything was first on her list of things she *had* to do right away, like go to Stevie's, then to Laura's, then to Meg's. Like run to her own house and hurl herself against the front door. Like hug every tree on Half Moon Lane.

"Look, Mrs. Plumley's in her kitchen!" Molly squealed, as if their elderly neighbor were standing on her head instead of just opening her refrigerator. "And the Toths cut down their big pine tree," Molly noticed.

Mr. Quindlen clicked his tongue in mock horror. "Well, I guess they should have checked with us out in Kansas first before doing that! Let's give 'em a toot and let 'em know what we think!" Mr. Quindlen beeped the feeble horn of the compact car all the way up the driveway.

"At least our house still looks the same," Molly breathed when she saw the friendly windows of 31 Half Moon Lane. "Omigosh, somebody's in there!" With that, Molly unbuckled her seat belt, scrambled over Scotty, and was out of the car before Mr. Quindlen turned off the engine.

"Surprise! Surprise!" Stevie cried when Molly got to the front door where a big WELCOME HOME banner stretched across the top. "You saw my head pop up, didn't you?"

"How could I miss it?" Molly laughed, patting Stevie's rumpled strands of reddish blonde hair and hugging her over and over.

"We've been looking after the house since Mrs. Hansen left for her son's a couple of days ago," Mrs. Ames explained when the girls finally untangled themselves from each other. "Stevie's been lying on that couch for an hour while we waited for your car to pull up. She somehow thought it would be a great idea to leap out at you in the dark, but I managed to convince her to at least leave the lights on."

"Glad you did, Judy," Mr. Quindlen said gratefully. "I don't know if I could have survived the scare after such a long trip." He picked up Stevie and whirled her around the living room. "So this is who's been haunting our house!"

In no time the house was filled with voices all talking and laughing at the same time as everyone trooped in and out to bring in all the luggage, bags, presents, and odds and ends from the long airplane trip.

"Here, I brought you these, Stevie." Molly reached into her jacket pocket for a cellophane bag containing plastic pilot's wings and a foil-wrapped after-dinner mint from the plane meal.

"Neat-o," Stevie said. She loved the presents, but was especially overjoyed at the best present of all, Molly Quindlen. "Hey, great. You wore the T-shirt," Stevie cried when she noticed what Molly was wearing under her jacket. "Looks like we shrunk!"

"It *is* a little smaller than when I left, but I wear it all the time, anyway," Molly said. She pulled and stretched the photo T-shirt the Friends 4-Ever had given her on her very last day before going to Kansas. Imprinted on the front was a now-blurry image of Stevie, Meg, and Laura smiling huge smiles right across the shirt.

"Thanks to that shirt half of Cross Plains knew you girls before you ever came out last summer," Mr. Quindlen told Stevie.

"She doesn't let me launder it very often," Mrs. Quindlen added. "She's afraid I'll wash you away! Now, come over here, Stevie Ames, and let me get a good look at the real you. You've certainly changed since you had your picture taken for that shirt."

"She has not, Mom," Molly insisted. Still, she

couldn't help noticing that Stevie seemed to be taller than she was. Maybe Stevie just had tall hair or tall sneakers or something.

"Same eleven freckles," Stevie announced. She certainly hoped all this fussing would be over soon so she and Molly could get on with the important stuff like calling Laura and Meg and going up to Molly's room. It would take the whole night to tell Molly about all the plans they had to fill up every second of the next few weeks.

"Same old Stevie," Mrs. Quindlen sighed, hugging her again. "Now, why don't you girls go upstairs with Molly's bags and some of her other things, while your mother and I catch up with each other?"

Molly gathered up various plastic shopping bags while Stevie tried to lift two duffel bags. "What'd you bring, Molly, the whole state of Kansas?"

"Not half of what she wanted to bring, Stevie," Mr. Quindlen laughed. "We almost had to charter a private plane! Here, let me help you with those."

After Stevie and Mr. Quindlen went upstairs, Molly got a strange, floaty feeling. Now that most of the luggage was put away, she took a long look at the living room. It seemed so bare, so tidy compared to the memories she had filed away of her old house. All the Quindlens' *real* furniture was still in a warehouse until they came back to Rhode Island for good. This living room belonged to someone who didn't play Battleship or wear muddy sneakers or leave little plastic people under the couch.

"Hey, Molly," Stevie shouted down the stairs. "What're you doing down there?"

"Nothing," Molly whispered, but *something* about the simple, bare room bothered her. She was in her house, but it didn't belong to her anymore.

Stevie rode down the banister and landed with a crash where Molly was standing. "C'mon. We have to get Laura and Meg over here. I promised I'd call them right away, and time's a-wasting."

Molly climbed the steep carpeted stairs slowly. They were so different from the wooden ones in her grandpa's house, which twisted and turned until you finally got to the top. Molly paused outside her room.

"My mom was right," she began. "They are pink."

"What are pink?" Stevie wanted to know.

"The wallpaper houses. I almost forgot."

"You should have asked. I would have told you in a letter," Stevie said. "Or taken a picture. Hey, that gives me a great idea, a Meg Milano

41

kind of idea. Why don't we take pictures of your whole house, the rooms and everything, while you're home, so you'll remember everything when you go back to Kansas?"

A cloud passed over Molly's face.

"Sorry, Molly, I'm so dumb," Stevie stammered. This was no time to think about going back to Kansas. "You just got here. Listen, I'm going to go downstairs and call Meg and Laura. They'll be so jealous I was here first."

Molly heard Stevie gallop down the stairs again. She looked around her old room and touched the wallpaper houses. She and the Friends 4-Ever, when they were just four plain-old friends, used to pretend that mouse families lived in the houses. Molly stooped down in a corner by the window.

"They'll be here in less than a minute," Stevie said when she bounded back into the room. "If you're checking for dust balls, forget it. Unless you want to come to my room, of course. But Mrs. Hansen's super neat." Stevie giggled. "Neat as in nice and neat as in no dust balls."

"Take a look here," Molly said, pointing to some faint pencil lines way down in the corner of the room. "Remember when we used to play mouse family and we drew paths and roads between the houses in this corner?"

"Oh, yeah," Stevie said, but she wasn't one to remember things that happened when they were five — especially if they involved imaginary mouse families. "Know what I liked best? The secret messages you left for us around the house when you went to Kansas. Remember how Mrs. Hansen found them and showed me where they were? Whenever I got behind on my letter writing, which happened a lot, I'd come over and read them. That always got me in the writing mood." Stevie grinned.

"Let's go find the messages," Molly said. "I sort of feel like this isn't my house anymore, you know?" How could she explain to Stevie how weird everything seemed? The only things that belonged to her were the wallpaper and the secret messages. This was Mrs. Hansen's room now with a sewing table and a narrow daybed and pictures of children Molly didn't know scattered about the room.

Stevie opened the closet and carefully pushed aside Mrs. Hansen's clothes. "Here it is, the first one Mrs. Hansen found."

There in Molly's neat rainbow printing was the message:

REMEMBER ME WHEN THIS YOU SEE !
Molly

"C'mon," Stevie said, grabbing Molly's hand. "There's another one in the closet in your parents' bedroom."

The girls stooped down to the baseboard in the big walk-in closet and read Molly's old message to her friends.

No matter where,
No matter how far,
Molly's heart
Is where her best friends are.
Friends 4-Ever,
Molly

"And her best friends are . . . right here!" Meg Milano screamed, making Molly and Stevie jump with fright.

"Surprise!" Laura said, squeezing herself into the closet, too.

Meg and Laura hugged Molly and wouldn't let her go.

"Hey, it this a private party or can anybody come?" Stevie cried, wedging herself into the circle of huggers.

"You're back, you're back," Laura kept repeating. Her brown eyes sparkled and her long, dark hair tickled Molly's cheek.

"Hey, wouldn't this closet make a great clubhouse?" Meg laughed, showing both her dimples. "Of course, we'd have to clear out Mrs. Hansen's clothes, but otherwise it's perfect."

"Or maybe we could meet in a shoebox or in the medicine cabinet, Meg," Stevie said, practically suffocating in the closet.

"Never mind Stevie," Molly said to Meg. "If it weren't for you, there wouldn't even be a Friends 4-Ever Club. I read all the letters you wrote a million times. A zillion."

Meg was beaming, and her gold hair was falling over her face. "Oooo," was all she could say. But she was proud that she was the one who had gotten their special friendship club organized with a name, and letters, and emergency meetings.

"Do we have to stay huddled in this closet for the rest of the night?" Stevie wanted to know. "I can't breathe in here."

"Yeah, let's go to Mrs. Hansen's sewing room, I mean Molly's room," Laura stammered quickly, realizing how awful that must sound.

"Yes," Meg said. "We have a list of all the things we have planned for every minute you're here, Molly. We're having an important Friends 4-Ever meeting first thing tomorrow morning. Then Monday you're coming to school with us since we're not out yet, boo-hoo. You can watch us make fools of ourselves rehearsing for our *St. George and the Dragon* play."

"But I have to go visit my Aunt Peggy and Uncle Ted for a couple of days," Molly protested. "In New Hampshire. My parents are leaving Monday."

But that didn't stop Meg. "Relatives? No way," Meg said. "It's not on my list, so you can't go. Besides, we arranged everything with Mrs. Courtney, the principal. She's got a visitor's badge ready for you and everything."

"You're staying at my house," Stevie said. "My mom said so."

"Okay," Molly said meekly. She could see there was no use arguing, and maybe going to her old school would be fun.

"Now, where's my clipboard?" Meg wanted to know. "Oh, I think I left it in your room."

"With her badge and her police whistle," Stevie whispered in Molly's ear.

In their excitement, the girls bumped into each other as they squeezed out of the closet and bumped into each other again when they all tried to fit into Molly's bedroom doorway. When they finally got through, each of the girls found her special corner.

Stevie, Meg, and Laura all exchanged not-so-secret glances.

46

"What's up, guys?" Molly wanted to know.

"A surprise," the three other girls said at the same time. "You'll find out tomorrow when Stevie comes to get you. Nine o'clock sharp, okay?"

"Okay," Molly agreed. This whole day had been surprise enough. "Now I have a surprise for you! One that was here the whole time I was gone."

Three pairs of eyes opened wide.

"What is it?" Meg asked, surprised at any surprise she hadn't personally planned herself.

Molly got up and went to the window seat and slowy lifted the lid. "You guys missed this one."

The girls scrambled over to the window and hunched down to see what Molly was talking about. In the same familiar rainbow handwriting they began to read:

When I return,
This message we'll read
The four of us
Are all we need.

Friends 4- Ever,
Apart and Together
Molly

47

THE FRIENDS 4-EVER
RESCUE PLAN

"What's that thud at the back door?" Mrs. Quindlen asked as she spooned cocoa into a pan of simmering milk.

"A thud like that could only be one thing — Hurricane Stevie," Mr. Quindlen joked.

Molly jumped up from her place at the kitchen table and ran to open the door for her friend.

"Brr. It's cold out there," Stevie said through chattering teeth as she stepped into their kitchen. "I wish people didn't expect newspapers when it snows. I had an extra. Sorry it's wet, Mr. Quindlen," she said, hurling a damp bundle to Molly's dad as if it were a football. "I wish I never told my brother Mike I'd take over his paper route on bad days. Even if I do get paid extra for getting soaked."

The Quindlens smiled at the sight of a very wet, snow-covered Stevie whose red cheeks matched her red jacket. She stomped her feet a few times on the mud rug, then stepped out of her too-big boots.

"So are you the one responsible for all that white stuff out there, Stevie Ames?" Mr. Quindlen asked.

"Not me!" Stevie protested. "Meg was the one who kept saying wouldn't it be great if it snowed when Molly came back. She probably organized the whole thing!" As she rubbed her hands together and hopped up and down to warm her feet, Stevie tried hard not to stare at the huge plate of cinnamon-dusted doughnuts in the middle of the Quindlens' table.

"Help yourself," Mrs. Quindlen told Stevie when she saw her hungry expression. "I'm just making hot chocolate for Molly and Scotty."

"I didn't know you helped Mike on his paper route," Molly said, impressed with Stevie's grown-up job.

"I'm saving up for a week of soccer camp next summer," Stevie announced proudly.

"Here's some hot chocolate to warm you up." Mrs. Quindlen set down a steaming blue mug in front of Stevie who immediately wrapped her fingers around the outside for warmth. "Mrs. Hansen even left a bag of miniature marshmallows and this little note."

> Dear Scotty and Molly,
>   Here's something sweet I keep in the house for my grandchildren and for my three favorite visitors, Laura, Meg, and Stevie. I thought you might like some of these to put in your own hot cocoa. I hope we get a chance to visit soon.
>
>   Love,
>   Mrs. Hansen

Molly, who had just been about to scoop a handful of the white puffs into her own cup, pushed away the bag as if the marshmallows had suddenly turned into bean sprouts. Everyone else was so busy watching what a huge pile of marshmallows Stevie was building in her cup, they didn't notice Molly crumple up Mrs. Hansen's note.

"Sounds as if you've been a pretty regular visitor here, Stevie," Mr. Quindlen observed. "Making sure Mrs. Hansen didn't have too many wild parties or race her motorcycle down the driveway while we were gone."

"Oh, Daddy." Even Molly had to laugh at her dad's joke. Though she hadn't met Mrs. Hansen, she knew from Stevie that she was an elderly lady who liked to do things like bake muffins and sew doll clothes.

"C'mon, Molly," Stevie said. "I'll show you her bell collection. We have a little time before our Friends 4-Ever meeting at Meg's. Mrs. Hansen has a story for each bell. Wanna see?"

"Not right now. I have to finish getting dressed," Molly told Stevie. She just couldn't understand how everybody could be so chummy with somebody who'd just moved in with her bell collection and sewing basket and took over Molly's *whole* house.

Stevie didn't insist. She was much too busy coating her spoon with as much melted marshmallow as she could skim off her hot chocolate to lick up. "Maybe later then," she told Molly. "You'll just love her collection."

After Molly got dressed, both girls layered on vests, extra socks, mittens, and scarves until they could hardly move. " 'Bye, see you later," Molly called out on her way to the front door. "We're going to Meg's. For a club meeting."

Stevie caught up to Molly and whirled her around. "Wrong way. We're taking the shortcut through your yard then over to Meg's. But first

I need you to close your eyes, and I'll guide you out."

"Whaaat?" Molly asked, puzzled and thrilled at the same time.

"I won't even ask what this is all about," Mr. Quindlen said when he peered over the top of his newspaper just as Stevie was leading Molly around an obstacle course of kitchen chairs. "I don't want to know."

Molly's eyes were shut tight. She heard the back storm door squeak open and felt cold air on her face. The fresh snow crunched underfoot when Stevie led her into the backyard.

"Okay, you can open your eyes now," Stevie said.

Molly blinked at the bright white light of the snow, then looked down. "The hammock! You put up our old hammock! I thought my mom threw it out when we went to Kansas. She said it was too faded and stringy and that we'd get another one when we came back. Where'd you find it?"

"At the curb on Junk Day after you left," Stevie said with a proud grin. "I took a few other things, too. Your rusty wagon and even some old coloring books." Stevie sat down softly on the old red-and-yellow-striped hammock and pushed herself off gently. "It made me feel like you were still here a little."

"Oh, Stevie. This is s-o-o nice," Molly said. Though the day was cold, Stevie's surprise made her feel warm all over. And though the hammock was pretty faded now, seeing it hang between her favorite tree and the dogwood in the corner of her yard brought back memories of wonderful summers with her three best friends. For a few minutes the two girls swung gently, swooshing their boots beneath the hammock until they wore away the new snow clean to the ground.

"Hey, you two! Time for our meeting," Meg's voice called from a couple of backyards away. "C'mon. We have to get started."

Molly and Stevie dug their heels into the ground to stop the hammock. "I'll get out first, then pull you," Stevie said, remembering that getting into a hammock was a lot easier than getting out.

With Stevie leading the way, the two girls found the opening in the privet hedge at the back of the Quindlens' yard, then scooted through another secret passage in the thick hemlock bushes that separated Meg's yard from her neighbor's.

"Eee! I just got snow down my neck," Molly said as she carefully parted the brittle branches so she wouldn't break them. She tried to brush the snow away from her jacket collar, but that only sent more snow down her neck.

"Come on, come on," three voices urged her from the other side of the hedges.

When Molly finally got through the tangle of cold branches, her three friends were standing there with identical wait-till-you-see-this expressions. "Ta dah!" they sang as they stood in a line and pointed to the middle of Meg's big backyard.

"Omigosh! You put up the tent for our clubhouse! I don't believe it," Molly said in disbelief. The Milanos' big orange tent the girls used as the summer clubhouse looked like something that had floated down from outer space into the snowy yard.

"I had to beg my parents to let me put it up. You should have heard my father grumbling and complaining while he tried to hammer the tent pegs into the ground. It's hard as a rock," Meg said proudly now that the job was down. "We can only leave it up for today. The cold's not good for nylon zippers."

"And there's no heat except for us," Stevie laughed.

"We had our very last Friends 4-Ever meeting with the four of us in there, remember, Molly? The day before you left?" Laura said softly. "I guess this is a coming-back party," she told her friend.

"Well, let's go in and warm up," Meg suggested.

"Yeah, Meg, I bet it's ninety degrees in there," Stevie said. "I just wish I'd brought my bathing suit and flippers."

Laura and Molly just couldn't stop giggling while Meg unzipped the front flaps and Stevie tried to think of more wisecracks.

"Let's leave our boots out here," Meg told the girls. "So we don't make puddles inside."

"Or ice," Stevie joked as she pulled off her brother's hand-me-down boots and left them outside the door of the tent.

When Molly got inside, she felt sure she had never been in a cozier place in her life. Meg had thought of everything, including the thick camping mattress spread out on the tent floor. "Ooo, this is just great," Molly said, feeling warmer already. The orange walls and ceiling made the whole tent feel sunny and bright, though just outside its thin walls it was a gray winter day.

When everyone was seated cross-legged in a

circle, Meg whisked a paisley scarf off a glass ball candle holder.

"Our crystal ball from the Gypsy Club!" Molly shrieked.

"Now don't get upset thinking about your bad luck fortune the last time we played Gypsy Club," Laura told Molly. "This time it's going to be different."

Everyone looked at Meg who was pounding a hammer against her clipboard. "I hereby call the meeting of the Friends 4-Ever to order," she said, starting this meeting just like all the other club meetings the girls had held over the years. "Today we will begin with fortune-telling."

"Oh, do we have to?" Molly moaned. "I already know my fortune. Or misfortune. My plane ticket back to Kansas."

Meg pounded the little hammer. "No, no. We've got a brand-new fortune for you, Molly. So just sit and listen, okay? Laura will go first."

Laura leaned over and swirled her hands over the glass ball. "I see a girl with brown hair and bangs, no, not bangs, and she's lying in a sleeping bag in Meg Milano's bedroom." Laura giggled and pretended to concentrate on the glass ball while she sneaked a peek at Molly. "I see the same girl eating dinner at my house. Breakfast, too."

Molly was a little disappointed. She'd already figured on plans for sleepovers and having dinner with her friends during her visit. She knew that without any fortune-telling.

Laura moved away from the glass ball, and Stevie took her place. "I see . . ."

Meg pounded the hammer again. "Stevie! You have to rub the ball first!"

"Oh, right, right." Stevie made exaggerated hand motions over the glass ball then began again: "I see, mmm, I see an empty space in the Milanos' china closet. A thief has stolen a glass candle holder!"

"Stevie, cut it out!" Meg ordered, banging her little hammer furiously. "You have to follow the plan."

"Okay, okay. *This* prediction is for real," Stevie said more seriously. "I see Molly living at my house for the next few months and not going back to Kansas!"

"If only," Molly sighed. "What's your prediction, Meg?" Maybe Meg would come up with something more likely to happen.

Meg swirled the scarf a few times over the ball and paused until everyone was sitting still. "I see Friends 4-Ever on an important mission to keep Molly in Rhode Island. I see . . . success!"

"And I see my parents saying forget it, just

like last time," Molly said. "Don't you remember how many times I asked them if I could live with you guys and how many times they told me I couldn't?"

"This is different!" the other three girls cried out together.

"Don't you see, Molly?" Meg began. "Your parents already told you they're coming back next summer, right? That's only a few months away."

"Almost six months," Molly mentioned, but Meg wasn't the least bit bothered by this detail.

"Okay, six months. But that's not so long," Meg said.

"In the middle there's a two-week spring vacation. You can see your family in Kansas then," Stevie said, as if Molly's flying out to see her parents would be a cinch.

Molly couldn't help it. She actually perked up a little. She got an old feeling she often had in the tent when they used to meet — a feeling that anything they cooked up in there had a chance of happening. Maybe staying in Crispin Landing wasn't so crazy.

"I already talked to Mrs. Courtney, the principal," Meg said, proud of herself for speaking to a grown-up about this plan. "She said sometimes kids stay with relatives if their real families have to move someplace before school gets out."

"But you're not my relatives," Molly pointed out.

Meg looked a little hurt at Molly's doubts. "Well, we practically are! I know I can figure out something." At that moment, no one doubted that Meg could.

For the next half hour, the four girls worked on the Friends 4-Ever Rescue Plan, as they called it. Or F.F.E.R.P., as Stevie nicknamed the mission. They were to begin that very day dropping hints to all their families about how awful it was that the Quindlens had to go back to Kansas. Step two was Molly's visit to Crispin Landing Elementary. When her parents saw how much she missed her old school, they were sure to go along with the Rescue Plan.

"Now, no begging and no whining," Meg warned. "That's going to be the hard part, but the plan won't work if we act like babies. We have to make our parents kind of think it's *their* idea. That's what the twins on *All Grown Up* did when they wanted their parents to let them go to a New Year's Eve party. I just know we can make this work," Meg said, putting away the glass ball. She certainly didn't need its special powers to make the Rescue Plan happen.

"So what do you think?" Laura asked Molly eagerly.

Now that the meeting was breaking up, Molly's flicker of hope sputtered out. It would never work. But when she looked at her friends' glowing faces, she knew she couldn't tell them that or of the thoughts about Kansas she was having. Thoughts about her grandpa, Kristy, Chocolate, and even the wagon train project that was due in history when she got back from vacation. "It's great," she said, but she didn't quite believe her own words.

"Now that we've got Molly's life all planned out, can we have some hot chocolate?" Stevie wanted to know.

Laura carefully unscrewed the top of a gray metal thermos and slowly poured the steaming chocolate into four plastic cups.

"Let's make a toast," Meg said. "To Molly and the Friends 4-Ever Rescue Plan."

"To F.F.E.R.P.," Stevie added.

The girls touched cups and sipped the warm drink.

"To Molly!"

TAGALONG

For three whole days, the girls did a good job of turning whatever conversation their parents were having into a discussion about what a good time Molly was having, if only she didn't have to go back. Though it wasn't easy to keep from adding, "Can Molly live with us?" they didn't say it.

For Stevie, Meg, and Laura, everything their parents said seemed like a sign that the Friends 4-Ever Rescue Plan was working. Laura's parents said, yes, it was a shame the Quindlens had to go back to Kansas. Mrs. Ames told Stevie she understood how hard it would be for Molly to leave her friends a second time. And the Milanos even agreed with Meg that six months was a long time to wait for Molly to come home for good.

Molly was the only one who didn't see any signs that the Rescue Plan was moving along. In fact, her parents warned that even going for a visit to Crispin Landing Elementary School might not turn out the way she expected. "It might be hard just sitting on the sidelines," her mother had said.

On Monday morning, the day of the school visit, Molly was determined to prove her parents were wrong. She was going to *love* going back to her own school, and the only thing that could possibly spoil the visit was the fact that she had nothing to wear.

Mrs. Hansen wouldn't have recognized her sewing room if she had walked in when Molly was trying on different outfits. "I brought all the wrong things," Molly repeated with every piece of clothing she flung on the floor. And the tops! How could she have thought the cowgirl-style flannel shirt she loved in Kansas would ever look right in Rhode Island? She balled up the shirt and aimed it into the far corner of her room. "All I need is a lasso to go with *that*!"

"Mom, where are my turquoise sweatpants?"

she called down the hall where her mother was helping Scotty with *his* clothes.

"In the laundry bag," Mrs. Quindlen yelled back.

"What?" Molly cried. They hadn't even been in Rhode Island long enough to get their clothes very dirty.

"In the laundry bag. Back home in Kansas. Remember I said everything you wanted to bring had to go into the laundry by last Monday at the latest?"

Unfortunately Molly remembered. She had missed the turquoise sweatpants deadline, and now she had nothing to wear.

Mrs. Quindlen came into Molly's room to see what the groans were all about. "What's all this?" she asked, surveying the piles of jeans, tops, and pajamas lying in heaps all over the room.

"I packed all the wrong things!"

"What do you mean? What's wrong with this?" Mrs. Quindlen asked, holding up a boring red sweater. "With that plaid shirt over there?" she nodded toward the rejected cowgirl shirt.

"Never mind, Mom, I know what I want," Molly groaned, though she knew nothing of the kind. If only she had thought ahead about having to face all the kids at Crispin Landing Elementary.

"You know, you can still come with us to Aunt Peggy's this afternoon, Molly," her mother said. "Uncle Ted says there's a couple of feet of snow at Buttermilk Mountain. You and Scotty could try skiing. It might be fun."

"I want to have fun here," Molly whined before she remembered Meg's no-whining rule.

"Okay, okay, but if you change your mind, we're going at noon in case you decide to leave school early," Mrs. Quindlen said. "Do you have your things all packed for Stevie's?"

"Almost," Molly fibbed. Every single thing she had brought to Rhode Island was scattered somewhere in the room. "Anyway, Stevie's mom has the key, and she can let me in if I forgot something. Good-bye, Mom. Yes, I know, you'll call me at Stevie's tonight," Molly added before her mother could get those words out herself.

"At least I have my ears pierced," she consoled herself after shooing out her mother. She pressed her earlobes to make sure her tiny horseshoe studs were firmly anchored. Maybe those and her mother's oversized purple sweatshirt with the cow would look good with a pair of jeans.

"Yes, you can borrow it," Mrs. Quindlen sighed when Molly ran across the hall to her parents' bedroom and rummaged through the closet for the sweatshirt.

"Thanks, Mom. It's nice and big, like all the kids wear," Molly said. "And the cow on the front is sort of cute."

By the time the Quindlens' doorbell rang six times in a row, Molly was ready to face her friends.

"Oh, c-u-u-u-te," Meg and Laura cried when Molly answered the door in her borrowed outfit.

"You look great!" Meg said. "I guess I'll never be allowed to get *my* ears pierced."

"How about your nose?" Stevie broke in, impatient with all this ooing and ahhing over sweatshirts with cows and ears with holes in them. "Let's go, already! I've got to practice my fire breathing."

Meg and Laura had to laugh. "Stevie's only got about twelve lines in the *St. George and the Dragon* play for the holiday concert, and half of them are roars," Meg explained to Molly. "She wouldn't try out for something sweet like *The Magic Princess*, but she couldn't wait to be a dragon!" Meg rolled her eyes in disbelief.

Stevie blew a whoosh of air in Molly's face and bared her teeth. *"I am the Dragon, here are my jaws! I am the Dragon, here are my claws!''*

The girls giggled. ''No tears over this play,'' Laura told Molly. ''We all have parts this time.''

''I'm the Hobby Hoss,'' Meg said proudly. ''I get to come on first and wear a humongous white cardboard horse costume. Do you remember it, Molly?''

''Sure I do,'' Molly told her friends. What she didn't say was that being in *St. George* was one of the things she had given up when she went out to Kansas, and it made her very sad. The short play was part of a holiday tradition at Crispin Landing Elementary, and the older kids performed it for the younger ones every year. Molly was one of those older kids now, but of course, she couldn't be in the play.

Laura sensed just what Molly was feeling. As they walked down Half Moon Lane, she stayed back with Molly, as Stevie pretended her frosty breath was fire and Meg galloped away in terror down the street. ''What kinds of holiday stuff did your school do in Cross Plains, Molly?''

''Well, I was going to play Laura in a Christmas scene from one of the *Little House* books, remember? Only now Tammy's playing my part.''

''I can't even picture it,'' Laura said. ''Remember how she and her friends in the Terrible Three

66

treated us like babies when we went out to visit you last summer? I can't believe she could play a part that was meant for you."

"I know. I can hardly stand it. It's going to be hard to have to listen to her brag when I go back."

"But you're not going back," Laura said. "Not if we can help it. Meg thinks now that all our parents keep saying how it's too bad you have to go back, that maybe you won't."

"You don't understand. It's not that easy," Molly said, but she stopped before she felt any worse. Today was supposed to be a fun day, not a crying day. "Tell me about your part in *St. George*," Molly asked before she got more upset.

"Well," Laura began. "This time Meg and Stevie have the big parts. I'm just a basket dancer."

"You mean you weave in and out, sort of the way a basket is made?" Even though Molly hadn't seen *St. George* for a long time, she remembered how much she had admired the older girls who did all the complicated steps of the basket dance without getting tangled up. Now Laura was going to be one of them.

"We can't seem to get it right no matter how many times Mrs. Walker shows us," Laura complained. "I'm the only one who takes dance, so it's easy for me. But some of the other girls! They move around like they're learning how to walk."

Laura's last words were lost in the roar of squeaky school bus brakes and impatient car horns that greeted the girls when they got to the busy corner of Crispin Landing Road and Warburton Avenue. The intersection was a jumble of kids and cars rushing to work and school. It was so different from the small school Molly attended in Kansas. For a minute she felt homesick, but not for this huge-looking school she didn't go to anymore.

"Hey, Joe Pat, look who's here," Stevie said to the crossing guard.

"Who?" the man asked, studying Molly's face while half the drivers in Camden waited for him to wave them on.

"Molly Quindlen, of course," Stevie announced. But Joe Pat looked completely baffled.

"Never mind," Laura said to Molly when they finally reached the other side. "He pays more attention to cars than he does to us. We might as well be sheep."

"Or cows," Meg said, sounding as if she planned to report Joe Pat to the traffic department for not recognizing her friend.

"Or hippos," Stevie said, waddling toward the school.

Molly laughed and tried hard not to feel hurt that Joe Pat didn't know who she was. It *had* been a long time.

"Come on, Molly." Meg tugged at her hand. "We have to check you into the principal's office first and get a visitor's badge for you."

"Not that you're really a visitor, of course," Laura explained. "It's just some dumb rule, that's all."

By the time Molly pressed on the metal bar of the lobby door, she wasn't at all sure anymore that going back to her old school was such a good idea. Joe Pat's blank look and the crowds of kids knocking their backpacks into her gave her a scary first-day-of-school feeling.

"Don't you just love being back?" Meg said, rushing down the hall with Molly at her heels.

Thank goodness Meg didn't expect an answer because everything was a blur of motion and noise to Molly right then. She wished she'd never come.

"We have to leave you here, Molly," Meg explained when they finally reached the principal's office. "Just tell them you're a visitor with our class. They already know. Then come straight to room 32. Hey, are you okay?"

Before Molly could answer, Meg, Stevie, and Laura had melted into the crowd of kids rushing to beat the second bell. When it rang, Molly was alone in the silent hallway.

Turning into the principal's office, Molly was relieved to see a familiar face. Mrs. Van Tassel, the school secretary, was stapling papers at the tall counter that separated the waiting area from the rest of the office.

Molly walked up to the counter. "Hi, Mrs. Van Tassel."

Mrs. Van Tassel pushed down her reading glasses and peered down at Molly from the counter. "May I help you, dear?"

"It's me, Molly. Molly Quindlen, remember?" she said in a quavery voice.

Before Mrs. Van Tassel had a chance to answer, a teacher Molly didn't recognize rushed up to the counter. "Eleanor, did you get a chance to run off those math sheets?"

"The copier's broken again," Mrs. Van Tassel began before going into a long explanation about how it wouldn't be fixed for two days and why didn't the teacher come back then.

Molly put down her backpack and sat down on the waiting bench while the two women complained about the broken copier. After a long time, Molly wondered if the clock in the office was broken, too. Even if she got the visitor's badge right this minute, she was still going to have to walk into her friends' class after everybody was settled down to work. She could just picture kids looking up and wondering who was this girl with a badge and the weird cow shirt.

When the teacher finally left, Molly waited for Mrs. Van Tassel to call her up to the counter. Instead she heard the woman begin typing. She had completely forgotten about Molly!

Maybe I'll go home, Molly thought. I'll tell Stevie, Laura, and Meg I changed my mind and decided to go to New Hampshire after all.

Just as Molly was putting on her jacket, Mrs. Van Tassel leaned over the counter, her face full of embarrassment and apology. "Oh, dear, I'm so sorry. Everybody wants something in a hurry this morning. Now tell me how I can help you. Is this your first day?"

Molly struggled with her jacket, which was half on and half off. "No, well . . . I'm just visiting, but I changed my mind."

Mrs. Van Tassel's face lit up suddenly. "Molly Quindlen! I recognize you now. I've just been in such a tizzy this morning with that copier. Everybody seems to think I should be able to fix it myself," the woman went on, getting herself all worked up again. "Well, never mind that, let me get a good look at you." She came around the counter to inspect Molly. "Your hair's different, isn't it? No more bangs. You're a whole other child! Makes me feel old the way you children keep growing like weeds when you couldn't even put your boots on alone not so long ago."

Molly looked around. She hoped no one she knew would think she was someone who couldn't get her boots on. Why, in Kansas she not only wore real riding boots every day, but she rode a horse as tall as the office counter. Taller even!

"Can I get my visitor's badge?" she asked as soon as Mrs. Van Tassel stopped to catch her breath.

"Of course, it's right here, all filled out thanks to Meg Milano. She must be an awfully good friend, Molly. She came in here several times last week to make sure I would have it ready for you."

"Thanks," Molly said when Mrs. Van Tassel finally pinned on the badge.

"One more thing. You need this note," the woman said, handing Molly a yellow piece of paper. "I'm afraid your friends have a substitute teacher today who may not be expecting you."

Molly tried not to groan out loud. A substitute! They were the worst. If Mrs. Van Tassel hadn't given her a soft push toward Meg's and Stevie's classroom, Molly would have run out of the building right then. "Go on now, have a good time," the woman said to Molly.

When she got to room 32 Molly stood in front of the door for a minute. Was she supposed to knock or just go in? She knocked softly just to make sure, then slowly opened the door.

Every head in the room turned toward Molly when she walked in. If only she could make herself evaporate. The students' faces were all a blur, except for Meg and Stevie who were trying to wave without getting caught. Molly walked up to the big desk and handed over her note to an impatient-looking man.

"That's all I need, a visitor," he muttered to himself, but of course the whole class heard him. "Well, go find a seat."

Molly walked to the only empty desk in the room, which tilted because one of its supporting legs was broken. Everyone was busy writing on some kind of worksheet except for Molly. For forty minutes, she sat there with nothing to do except try to figure out who kids were from the back of their heads. She pulled out a clipboard and doodled for a while. Maybe she would write a letter to Kristy saying what a good time she was having. Except, of course, she wasn't.

Finally, the bell rang, and everyone stampeded out.

"Whew, do you believe it?" Meg said. "Of all days to get a substitute. Sorry, Molly."

"Now that we're out of prison, we can go to chorus," Stevie told Molly. "To rehearse *St. George*. Listen. I know all my lines. Rrrugh! Rrrugh!" She growled in her most dragonlike voice.

"Poor you, Molly," Laura said when she came over to the group. "You got Mr. Regan, the worst sub in Camden. Worse than Mrs. Higgle, even."

Molly joined the stream of kids going into the big music room. Maybe things would be a little more familiar in there.

Mrs. Walker, the music teacher, was up on the platform and waved Molly over. "Welcome back, Molly," she said, pushing away the permission slip Molly held out. "I could certainly use a good dancer like you over the next few days to get these basket dancers in shape. They seem to think of dancing as a contact sport. Tell me, how is Kansas? Have you been able to keep up with your ballet?"

Molly got all set to tell Mrs. Walker about how

she helped the gym teacher teach some jazz steps when Evan Rydell butted in. "Mrs. Walker, Mrs. Walker. Charles Stever took my shield and won't give it back."

Mrs. Walker put her hands on her hips and sighed. "Sorry, Molly. I hope I can catch you later. I do want to hear all about Kansas."

Within minutes, Mrs. Walker was busy coaching the kids who had speaking parts, while the basket dancers tried over and over not to run into each other. Molly didn't know quite where to sit or what to do, so she pulled up a chair next to the platform where Laura's group was. By now she had figured out who most of the kids were, though a lot of them had different haircuts and had gotten way taller than Molly remembered them. But practically no one seemed to remember her back. Except for a few small waves and a couple of "Hi's" everyone was busy with what they were doing.

"Who's he that seeks the Dragon's blood and calls so angry and so loud?" Molly heard Stevie shout out her lines on the other side of the room. In another corner, Meg pranced around yelling: *"Over mire and over moss, in comes I, the Hobby Hoss!"* And by the looks of things, Laura was beginning to get the basket dancers into shape

as she rewound the music tape and made her girls practice each step until they were ready for the next.

In the midst of all the music, foot tapping, and dragon roars, Molly had no lines to say and no steps to dance. She might as well have been a chair in the room. It was just too hard to stay here anymore doing nothing. So she decided to do something. She pulled her clipboard and pencil from her backpack and began to write.

Dear Meg, Stevie, and Laura,

The play looks great, and it was fun watching you. I decided that since you have a substitute today, I'm going to go to my Aunt Peggy's with my family for a couple of days after all. Sorry I'll miss the play.

Molly

Molly tucked her very un-Mollylike note in the front pocket of Meg's backpack and slipped out into the hall. Though the hall was quiet, Molly could hear the hum of the busy school as she passed by familiar rooms. When she went by the art room, she saw first-graders gluing cotton balls onto tree-shaped cones. In the science room, Mr. Retzloff, one of Molly's favorite old teachers, was doing something with a helium balloon. And when she passed the cafeteria, the warm smell of baked chicken brought back memories of sitting with Stevie, Laura, and Meg at lunch while they discussed whether it was a pudding day (yea!) or a baked apple day (yuck!). But the cotton-ball trees in art, the balloon experiment in science, and even the baked chicken all belonged to the *real* students at Crispin Landing Elementary School.

As the badge said, Molly was just a visitor.

PRICKLY PEARS

Thanks to Molly's New Hampshire visit, the Friends 4-Ever were nearly three days behind on the Rescue Plan — and on the long list of things they just *had* to do after Molly finally got back. Like making a log house out of bread sticks, for instance. The girls were up to their elbows in egg-white frosting and food coloring, and the Milanos' kitchen looked as if it would need to be rebuilt if the girls ever finished this project.

"I don't get it, Molly," Meg was saying as she carefully spread a layer of white frosting between two bread-stick logs. "I don't know how you could give up three whole days with us to go visit relatives." Meg said the word *relatives* as if

Molly's Aunt Peggy and Uncle Ted were reptiles or insects. "You missed *St. George* and my big starring part."

"I know, I'm sorry, Meg. Next year maybe," Molly said. "I hope so, anyway." How could she tell her friends how much it hurt to visit her old school and know she wasn't part of it anymore?

"You don't have to hope so, Molly," Meg told her. "The Rescue Plan is coming along great. Our parents, even my mom and dad, keep saying how they wish you could stay here for good. It's going to happen, I can feel it. I just wish we hadn't lost almost three days, that's all."

"Sorry," Molly said again. There was no use explaining why she went away. It would just hurt Meg's feelings, and she wouldn't understand, anyway.

"That's okay, Molly," Stevie said, helping herself to a candy cane. "You got to miss Evan Rydell stepping on my dragon tail twice while the play was going on!"

"And Rachel Garrity losing her costume bag!" Laura said. "She was the only basket dancer wearing jeans. I had to give her my shawl to tie around her waist so it wouldn't be so noticeable."

"Well, I'm just glad school's out now and

you're back," Meg said. "Now we can go ahead and do things together like we used to. We only have a few days before Christmas to finish this log house."

"Oh, so *that's* what this is!" Stevie said in fake amazement. "I hate to say it, you guys, but this doesn't look anything like the picture. I just hope we're better at keeping Molly in Rhode Island than we are at building gingerbread houses — if that's even what this is."

"Stevie, if you don't want to make a gingerbread house," Meg said, "then just say so."

"I don't want to make a gingerbread house," Stevie said. "I want to play ice hockey. This is the first day they've cleared the pond for skating since it snowed, and we're stuck in here making a gingerbread house that isn't even made out of gingerbread."

"It's a log house," Laura reminded Stevie. "We wanted to do something different this year, remember?" Even patient Laura looked a little tired of this Friends 4-Ever project. The bread sticks wouldn't stack up without sliding. The red cinnamon hearts had streaked into the white frosting, and the whole structure looked as if it were going to melt and crumble any minute.

"We just have to keep going," Meg told her

friends. "It'll look better once the frosting dries a little."

"Then maybe your Wheat Thin windows won't keep sliding down the side," Stevie said with a low chuckle.

By now the project was getting on everyone's nerves, especially Molly's. Like Stevie, she wanted to go out and get away from the mess, but Meg was determined to keep going just because it was on her list.

"The one I made with Kristy and her mom won a prize at our church last year," Molly mentioned as she tried to keep a graham-cracker shingle from slipping off the roof.

"Well, I guess the problem is we're not Kristy," Meg said.

"I didn't mean it that way," Molly apologized. "I just wanted to tell you about something I did in Kansas."

"Ever since you got back from New Hampshire, I've felt like you wished you were in Kansas with Kristy and those horses," Meg spit out.

Molly had nothing to say back. Meg was right, only she didn't know it. Since her visit to New Hampshire Molly *had* been talking about Kansas on purpose to make her friends see that she had to go back and that the Friends 4-Ever Rescue

Plan wasn't going to work. The Quindlens had four return plane tickets, and that was that.

"Sounds like you girls could all use some fresh air," Mrs. Milano said when she came into the kitchen and saw the gooey log house and the four girls glaring at each other. "That egg-white frosting works a little better when it's had some time to sit. How about if I take you ice-skating for an hour or so?"

"Saved!" Stevie cried in relief.

"I'd like to go skating," Molly said, hoping to get away from this sticky and unsuccessful project. "Kristy taught me to do some spins. We've had ice on our pond since Thanksgiving in Kansas."

"Goody for Kansas," Meg muttered under her breath.

"I'd like to go skating, too," Laura said.

"You can borrow my old skates, Molly," Stevie said. "I'm a size five now. I hope you don't mind that they're hockey skates."

"Thanks, Stevie. I wanted to bring my new white figure skates from home, but my dad said they wouldn't fit in my bag," Molly said, looking down at her own size-four feet. "Kristy knitted me some red pom-poms for the laces."

"Sorreee," Stevie said to Molly. "I'll go get my knitting needles."

Molly knew she was annoying her friends with her Kristy-this and Kristy-that talk, but she couldn't seem to stop herself. Somehow she had to make them see that Kansas was where she really lived now.

"Are you going skating, Meg?" Laura interrupted before Molly started in on more of this Kristy stuff.

"Maybe," Meg said, looking very much like she wanted someone to beg her to go.

"C'mon, Meg," Laura told her friend. "It'll be fun, and when we get back we can put the finishing touches on the cabin."

"Yeah, like most of the roof," Stevie broke in before Laura gave her a warning look.

"Well, okay," Meg grumbled, trying one last time to line up the corners of the log house so it stood straight.

The girls were glad to get away from each other for the few minutes it took to gather up extra mittens and socks and for Stevie to run home for the skates for Molly.

"You girls are awfully quiet," Mrs. Milano remarked on the way to the skating pond at Patriots Park. "I guess I didn't need my earplugs after all," she added a little later, but no one laughed.

In the backseat Molly stared out the window

while Laura braided the fringe on her scarf, and Stevie fiddled with the laces on her skates. Up front, Meg busied herself with cleaning out the glove compartment. Except for Mrs. Milano's comments about all the bad drivers who seemed to be out, no one said a word.

"Last stop," Mrs. Milano said when she pulled up in front of the recreation hall at the edge of the skating pond. "Here's some change, Meg, so you can call me when you girls are ready to come home. There's extra for all of you to get a snack."

"Thanks, Mrs. Milano," Molly said, finally breaking the silence as they got out of the car.

The pond was swarming with kids who had also just gotten word that the pond was finally ready for skating.

"Darn," Stevie said when she noticed the crowds squeezed onto a small circle of ice that had been shoveled off. "They didn't clear a section for hockey."

"That means more room for our kind of skating," Meg said, spinning in place.

"The no-hockey kind," Laura added when they went inside the recreation building to put on their skates.

The rest of Camden seemed to have the same

idea, and the girls had to wait a long time to find space on a bench.

"Ugh, I don't think these fit anymore," Meg groaned when she tried to squeeze a foot into the shoe of her right skate.

Molly looked down at the scuffed black hockey skates Stevie had lent her. She didn't know what to say without sounding ungrateful and just hoped the skates wouldn't fit.

"Here, let me tie them for you," Stevie said before Molly could come up with a little white lie. "Stand up and wriggle your foot. Should I tighten the laces a little more?"

"They're fine, Stevie, thanks." Molly had to admit they did fit perfectly. Too bad. She pulled down her jean cuffs as far as they would go and hoped no one would notice she was wearing old, black skates.

When all the skate-tying was done, the girls wobbled outside but tried to look as graceful as possible going down the wooden steps that led to the pond. As soon as they got on the ice, Stevie was off like a rocket, while Molly, Meg, and Laura looked around for a spot where they could skate together.

"It's pretty crowded," Laura said. "Let's stick together."

The girls slowly pushed off and tried not to fall as kids whizzed by them in every direction. Just when Molly felt fairly balanced, a boy in a scary-looking ski mask bumped into her and sent her flying into a group of older kids.

Laura and Meg slowly skated over and tried to help her up, but they were too unbalanced themselves.

"What's the matter, did you forget your double-bladed skates at home, little girl?" one nasty boy said to Molly.

"Knock it off, Koslow," Stevie said, when she streaked up to where Molly was sprawled out. "C'mon, take my hand."

Molly grabbed Stevie's wrist and tried to get up, then collapsed again, as the crowd of boys hooted. Laura and Meg came over and put out their arms to help Molly balance herself.

Molly felt as if every skater were looking at her as she tried to get up on the ice a third time. "There," she said, when she finally succeeded. "Boy, it sure is crowded here. Not like the pond we skate on at the Pollards'," she said to no one in particular, but of course Stevie, Meg, and Laura caught every word.

"Let's do a whip and show those jerks," Stevie suggested to cheer everybody up.

"There's no room for a whip," Molly pointed

out. "There's barely enough room skating by ourselves, and the ice is too bumpy and full of cracks," she said, hoping to convince her friends that the rough ice and crowds, not her wobbly legs, had made her fall.

"Not like Kansas, I suppose," Meg said, completely misunderstanding Molly.

"Yeah, I bet they have special ice smoothers out in Kansas," Stevie said, pretending to sweep the ice.

Although Laura didn't say anything, she stood by Meg and Stevie as if she were on their side.

"I'm going inside," Molly said. "These skates don't really fit."

"I suppose they're not as good as Kansas skates." Stevie looked mad and hurt at the same time.

Molly grabbed onto the branch of a tree at the edge of the skating pond and pulled herself off the ice.

"Where are you going, Molly?" Laura called out.

"Home!" Molly answered without turning around.

"Which is where? Kansas?" Stevie yelled at Molly's back as kids stood around watching the girls fight.

Molly whipped off her mittens and hat that

were making her itchy. "It's better than here!" she yelled back.

"Well, just go ahead!" Stevie shouted, while Meg and Laura looked on in horror at the sound of those terrible words.

Molly kept right on going toward the recreation building, slashing the snow with the blades of her skates as she rushed to get away from Stevie. When she was a foot away from the doors of the building, she felt something hard hit her back. Turning around, she caught Stevie getting another snowball ready.

"I bet they even have better snowballs in Kansas," Stevie taunted as she got ready to pitch.

With that, Molly hurled a chunk of snow from the snowbank and just missed Stevie's left ear. "They do! And they have sleigh rides and ice fishing and . . ." Molly couldn't go on. Big hot tears slid down her cold cheeks, and she shivered. She just wanted to go home.

Stevie dropped her deadly snowball to the ground and made her way toward Molly with Meg and Laura right behind. When they reached Molly, they guided her to a rock where she could sit down. They formed a huddle so no one would tease or stare at their crying friend.

"Oh, Molly, I'm sorry," Stevie said, "I don't even know why we're fighting or what's the matter, do you?" She rubbed away Molly's tears with the dry side of her woolly mitten.

Molly tried to speak, but nothing came out.

"I am *so* dumb, that's what's the matter," Meg said. "I started to figure it out when I saw you look so miserable when you fell on the ice and couldn't get up."

"Are you about to tell us for the millionth time about when you fell off that horse in Kansas, Meg?" Stevie said.

"And how you thought all those Kansas girls were making fun of you," Laura added.

"Well, I can't help it if it's true," Meg said. "Now the same thing's happening to Molly, only we're the ones who are making her feel out of place. We've been telling Molly to do this and do that and not giving her a chance to do what she wants."

"If only I knew what that was!" Molly wailed, finally finding her voice.

"Are you sorry you came back home?" Laura asked, shocked that she was even saying such a thing out loud.

"In a way," Molly admitted. "When you wrote to me about being in plays or having sleepovers and stuff, I pictured doing those things just like before. Only, I'm just a visitor, so the same old things aren't the same old fun."

Even Stevie stood there silently as Meg and Laura listened to Molly tell them how awful she felt.

"I can't stand thinking about going back, but I know I have to," Molly continued. "Going to school with you last Monday was the worst. I felt like a complete stranger. That's why I left."

The girls shivered, looking at their cold, miserable friend with the tear-streaked face.

"We don't know what to say," Meg began. "I mean, we thought the Friends 4-Ever Rescue Plan would be so great."

"I know," Molly agreed, "but it makes me feel worse to keep hearing about it."

Meg nodded, and Laura and Stevie just looked at their feet.

"Listen, I have to go wash my face or something. I feel all puffy," Molly said. "I'll come back out later."

"We don't have to skate," Stevie told her. "We could go back and work on the log house."

"Ugh, not that!" Meg said as if that were the worst idea in the world. "Whatever you want to do, Molly, that's what we want to do, too."

Molly took a deep breath and sniffled hard. "I'll be right back. Let's skate a little more, before we call your mom to pick us up."

Meg held out one hand and Stevie another to

pull Molly up from the rock where she had been sitting. Without looking up once, Molly made her way into the recreation building and went into the girls' room. She was glad there was no one in there to notice her splashing cool water onto her face and washing away her sadness. When her face felt better, she took a paper towel and dried it. Then she blew her nose as hard as she could. There. She almost felt like a normal person again.

Grabbing her hat and mittens, she threaded her way through the crowds of kids gathered in the building talking and fooling around. Now she knew what she wanted to do — just talk and fool around with her own friends.

When she got outside, she saw Meg, Stevie, and Laura trying to skate backward in the middle of the pond. Molly moved toward the pond, making her way carefully down the wooden steps that led to the ice. When she got to the bottom step she looked down and saw a message carved there.

WE'RE SORRY!
STEVIE, LAURA, MEG

THE BEST PRESENT OF ALL

The carols were sung, the stockings were empty, and all the aunts and uncles, cousins and friends had gone home. Molly was tired but wouldn't go to bed. She knew that when she did Christmas would be over. Instead she sorted and stacked, arranged and rearranged her presents on Mrs. Hansen's sewing table in her room.

She loved all her new presents, but what she loved best of all was a stick-on badge she was wearing that read: CRISPIN LANDING RESIDENT: MOLLY QUINDLEN.

"My mom has a stack of them from when the whole neighborhood had to go to the Town Hall to get a new traffic light on Warburton Avenue,"

Meg had explained when the girls gave Molly this odd present on Christmas Eve.

"We couldn't fit the traffic light in a box, so all you're getting is the badge," Stevie had joked.

"It's so you don't feel like a visitor anymore," Laura had told Molly.

Molly patted the badge now. She had worn it all Christmas Day, and when relatives and company asked what it was for, Molly had answered, "It's a membership badge."

And it was. Molly was a member of the best friends ever and the best neighborhood ever. Even living in Kansas didn't change that.

"I'll tell Kristy," she whispered as she ran her finger around the border of a new box of rainbow stationery her friends had also given her. "She'll understand."

Molly cleared a space on the sewing table and began to write.

Dear Kristy,
   Merry Christmas! Thanks for the little reindeer card and the pictures of the play.

You look beautiful, *and Tammy looks like a big show-off. (It was hard seeing her wearing my costume!)*

Sorry I didn't write to you sooner to tell you about what a good time I was having, except I wasn't!!!!

I was homesick. For two places! I miss you and Grandpa and horseback riding. This sounds weird, but I was also homesick for here, *even though I* was *here!!! When I visited my old school, I had to wear a badge! That was the worst.*

I had a big fight with my friends (Stevie hit me with a snowball!!!!), then we made up. And today they gave me a badge that says I'm a resident of our neighborhood. I've been wearing it all day because it makes me feel like I really fit in after all.

This is the first sheet of a new box of rainbow stationery my friends also got me for Christmas. They said it's a six-month supply until I come home for good. (I also got a mailbox with a lock and key for secret notes, a set of paintbrushes like real artists use, and a partridge in a pear tree — just kidding!!!! That was the last song we sang when we went caroling a couple of hours ago.)

In a way, I feel like I had two Christmases.

This one today and the one I know you're having in Cross Plains. I can just picture Starry Night and Chocolate wearing their sleigh-bell collars for the holiday. Did the birds find our wheat tree?

I just wanted you to know I miss you a lot and hope your Christmas is as good as mine turned out to be.

> *Merry Christmas and Happy New Year, too!!*

Molly

P.S. Could you give Chocolate a sugar cube for me?
P.P.S. Check the envelope before you throw it away!

With that, Molly tucked in the braided red-and-green friendship bracelet she had made for Kristy just a few days before. She folded her letter, put it in the envelope, stuck a stamp on it, and sealed it shut with her favorite holiday bear sticker.

She was still too wound up to even think about going to bed. Instead of getting into her pajamas, she took the letter and went downstairs to put it in the mailbox where Ed, the mailman, would be sure to pick it up first thing in the morning. Besides, she wanted one last look at their Christmas tree while it was still Christmas.

"You know, I miss our old ornaments," Mrs. Quindlen said when she caught Molly gazing at the tree from the stairway, "but it was so sweet of Mrs. Hansen to leave hers for us. The tree looks pretty, don't you think?"

Molly had to admit Mrs. Hansen's decorations looked sort of pretty, but she didn't have to admit it out loud, did she? "Mmm," was all she said as she reached for a candy cane from the tree.

"Caught ya!" her dad called out from the comfy chair where he was reading the new mystery Aunt Peggy had given him. "Couldn't sleep?"

"I'm tired, but I'm not tired," Molly said to her father, who nodded in agreement. Nobody wanted Christmas to be over just yet. "I'm mailing a letter to Kristy," Molly continued as she opened the front door and stuck her letter in the mailbox. "Hey, Mom, I think more company's coming," she whispered after she noticed an older woman walking over from Mrs. Plumley's next door.

Mrs. Quindlen quickly gathered up a few

strands of holiday ribbon and scraps of wrapping paper before going to the door. Molly couldn't help noticing her mother's big smile when she greeted the strange woman.

"Merry Christmas, Helen," she said, giving the woman a big hug. "Clara said you might stop by Crispin Landing when the excitement died down at your daughter's house."

"Merry Christmas to you, Debbie." The older woman removed a bright red shawl from her shoulders and put it on the side table with her purse and a small shopping bag of presents. "I hope it's not too late, but I wanted to see how you folks were getting along."

I was getting along fine until *you* got here, Molly thought, when she realized this nice woman was Mrs. Hansen, the Invader of Half Moon Lane. Molly wondered if there was any way she could hide in the corner by the fireplace then somehow sneak behind the couch and scoot up the stairs without being noticed.

"And you're Molly," the woman said, extending her hand out when she walked over to the wing chair where Molly had scrunched up. "I'm Mrs. Hansen, and I'm so glad to meet you at last."

Molly stood up and mumbled, "Hi."

"You know, it's so nice to match up your

pretty face with all the pictures your friends showed me. Especially that Stevie," Mrs. Hansen said with a chuckle. "I thought I had plenty of grandchildren to keep me from getting rusty, but Stevie is always a step ahead."

While Molly's parents shared a few of their own Stevie stories, Molly peeked at Mrs. Hansen. She didn't want to admit it, but just as Stevie had said, Mrs. Hansen *did* look a little like Mrs. Santa Claus in her red plaid skirt and red sweater. Molly couldn't stop staring at Mrs. Hansen's silver bell earrings that jingled every time she tilted her head or laughed, which was quite often.

"Do you like these?" Mrs. Hansen said when she noticed Molly looking at her ears. "My granddaughter gave them to me just this morning. You've probably seen my bell collection in the cabinet over there. Now these will be part of my display, too," she added, giving one of the earrings a jingle with her finger.

"Molly's kind of tired, Helen," Mrs. Quindlen explained when Molly didn't say anything. "She was just heading up for bed. Scotty's already sound asleep."

Molly knew her mother was just trying to give her a chance to make a getaway instead of standing there being unsociable, but now she seemed almost hypnotized by this person who had taken over her house. Some tiny part of her was beginning to understand why Stevie liked her so much.

"I *would* like to see your bell collection," Molly said shyly, when her voice finally came back. "Stevie said you had a story for each bell."

"Why, yes, I do," Mrs. Hansen said.

"I'll go make a pot of that nice orange spice tea you left for us, Helen," Mrs. Quindlen said, "while you and Molly get acquainted. Bill, maybe you could get some cups and saucers on a tray," she added, pulling Mr. Quindlen away from his chair so Molly and Mrs. Hansen could be alone.

Mrs. Hansen gently took hold of Molly's hand and walked her over to the tall china cabinet where her bells were displayed. She gave the key to the glass door a small turn so Molly could see and touch the bells.

"You know, I have so many favorites," Mrs. Hansen began before she pulled out a cream-colored bell trimmed with green holly leaves. "But I have to admit, this one is special. Would you like to try it?"

Molly reached out for the china bell and gave it a ring. "Hey," she said, "this says, 'Merry Christmas, Friends 4-Ever!' "

"Yes, it does," Mrs. Hansen said, running her finger over the gold writing on the bell. "Your friends gave this to me last year after I helped them make costumes for the play they were in. I heard that was one of your good ideas."

Molly beamed. "It was. Stevie was miserable about not being in the play with Meg and Laura. And she missed me."

"She certainly did," Mrs. Hansen said. "Why she never stopped talking about you the whole time you were gone. I think she liked visiting with me so much because it helped her feel close to you. And for me it was like having a granddaughter living just two doors down."

When Molly heard these words, she felt as if a ghost who had been haunting her house had just gotten up and gone out the door for good. The ghost of Mrs. Hansen, the Invader.

"Thank you for watching my house," Molly said, not mumbling in the least.

"And thank you for sharing it with me," Mrs. Hansen said back. "I'm certainly going to miss it when I move."

"Move! Who said anything about moving?" Mr. Quindlen bellowed when he came into the living room with a big tray of cups and saucers and Christmas cookies.

"Well, Bill, I know you folks will be coming

back to your own house one of these days. So I've started looking around a bit."

Molly felt a sharp stab of disappointment. She had just made a new friend, and now she was going to lose her. "Can't you stay in Crispin Landing?" Molly wanted to know.

Mrs. Quindlen's eyebrows went up in surprise at Molly's change of heart, then she smiled. "I see Mrs. Hansen must have shown you some of her magic bells, Molly."

Mrs. Hansen looked a bit puzzled, but Molly smiled a flickery sort of smile at her mother. She didn't want Mrs. Hansen to go. "What about the little house by the footbridge? The one with the empty bird cage the people left behind?"

The grown-ups looked puzzled. "When we went sledding the other day with Stevie's brothers, they said the house was empty," Molly explained. "Maybe you could rent that."

"Oh, I do know which house you mean, Molly," Mr. Quindlen said. "That's Mr. Fischer's old place. These girls know all the neighborhood gossip, who's moved in and who's moved out."

Soon the grown-ups were busy with their own gossip, which bored Molly silly since it was all about who had gotten married or divorced and not a word about any new nine-year-old girls moving in to the neighborhood. After taking one more candy cane, Molly went off to look at Mrs. Hansen's bell collection again.

One said Scotland, one said Arizona. There was one with blueberries on the front, which Molly knew came from Maine where Mrs. Hansen had lived before her husband died.

"You know, each of these bells came from people I've met in all the places I've lived and visited," Mrs. Hansen said when she noticed Molly's interest. "Now I even have one from here, from your friends."

Molly picked up the Friends 4-Ever bell and gave it another little ring, then another, and another — one jingle for each of her friends.

Mrs. Hansen put down her teacup and went over to the table in the hallway where she had put her things. "I have something here for each of you," she said, taking out several small wrapped gifts from her shopping bag.

"Oh, Helen," Mrs. Quindlen said.

"Well, I wanted to. You know you rented me your house and quite a few other things. But I can't pay you enough rent for the nice feeling this house has given me since I moved here, and now I want you to have something, too."

Molly's parents opened their box first. "Oh, this is so lovely, Helen." Mrs. Quindlen held up a Camden Centennial Spoon for her spoon collection. "I do miss my own things, I have to say. When we come back, I'm going to put this right in my own display cabinet."

"Go ahead, Molly, open yours," Mrs. Hansen urged.

Molly ran her finger under the Scotch tape and tried to do a careful job of removing the wrapping paper. She knew from Mrs. Hansen's closets that she was someone who not only collected bells but gift boxes, wrapping paper, and ribbons that could be used again. Like Molly, she was a saver.

"Ooo," Molly said when she opened the gift. Lying inside a red velvet box was a small china bell with a picture of the Old Dutch Church painted on it. Underneath were the words: *Camden, Rhode Island*.

"Now you'll have a piece of home and a little piece of me to bring back to Kansas," Mrs. Hansen said.

"I'll keep it right by my bed," Molly said, picturing exactly where she would put the bell in her Cross Plains bedroom. Just as Mrs. Hansen remembered a trip to Hawaii when she rang a hula-dancer bell, Molly would remember home when she rang her new bell.

"Thank you so much," Molly said, giving Mrs. Hansen a big hug. "I'll always think of you when I ring it."

Now she was ready to say good night to this year's Christmas. Molly climbed the stairs and turned around to take one last look at the glowing Christmas tree. She set the bell down on Mrs. Hansen's sewing table next to the rest of her gifts, gave a little egg-shaped wooden Santa a kiss good night, and jingled her new bell one more time.

"Merry Christmas, everyone."

8

HAPPY NEW YEAR,
EVERYBODY!

Molly was grunting and out of breath. She didn't
know a sewing machine could be so heavy.
When she set it down in the corner of her room
she was careful to move her feet out of the way
quickly so she wouldn't smash her toes.

"Whew!" she said when the room finally
looked ready for the Friends 4-Ever New Year's
sleepover. She had cleared the middle of the
floor for three more sleeping bags. Her dad had
brought up Mrs. Hansen's portable television set
from the den and plugged it in so the girls could
watch the New Year's ball drop at midnight. And
the sewing table, which Molly had pushed
against the wall, was a buffet of cookies, pop-

corn, chips, candy, soft drinks, party hats, and noisemakers.

As she caught her own breath, Molly heard a lot of huffing and puffing sounds coming up the stairs.

"You moving in, Meg?" Molly heard her dad say out in the hall.

"It's a sleepover, Mr. Quindlen," Meg answered, as if that explained why she was practically falling over from the weight of a sleeping bag, two pillows, a duffel bag, and an assortment of jam-packed shopping bags.

"Ooo, this looks great," Laura said, when she came into Molly's room. "Your room is almost like it was before you moved. Except for the TV, of course."

"If only," Meg sighed when she noticed the little TV all set up.

"Keep dreaming, you guys," Stevie said. "My mom says one TV a house is plenty."

"My mom thinks having a TV in the bedroom gives off poison vapors or something," Meg grumbled. "I guess I should just keep trying for a phone."

"It's a plot," Stevie said, "so forget it. All our parents got together and made up a no-TV-in-our-rooms rule."

The girls all sighed, but they were still pretty

happy that for one night, anyway, the no-TVs-in-bedrooms rule was suspended. Within minutes, they had unrolled their sleeping bags, fluffed and refluffed their favorite pillows from home, and wriggled into oversized T-shirts. Except for Molly.

"We should get you a new photo shirt before you go back," Meg said, noticing how tight the old one had become on Molly.

The room got quiet when the words "go back" sank in.

"Four more days," Laura said quietly. "I guess the Rescue Plan didn't work after all."

"Maybe we can think of a Friends 4-Ever Kidnapping Plan," Stevie added. "We'll leave a note telling your parents you disappeared in the middle of the night, and you'll be returned in six months."

Nobody laughed at Stevie's silly idea. In fact, everyone looked so gloomy all of a sudden, Molly felt sorrier for them than she did for herself. "It's okay. Honestly, I don't feel as terrible as I thought I would," she told her friends to cheer them up. "It's not forever like the first time I went. That's why I don't need a new T-shirt. I've got my stationery and Mrs. Hansen's bell and the three toys you gave me to help me last six more months. It's easier this time. Really."

"Not for us," Laura said sadly, and Meg and Stevie nodded in agreement.

"I know. Thanks, guys. It feels good knowing that you miss me so much," Molly said with a small smile. "But we should have fun tonight anyway and not think about four days away, okay?"

"Did somebody say fun?" Stevie asked suddenly as she grabbed a pillow.

"Pillow fight!" the girls all cried together when they heard Stevie's fighting words and saw a big pillow land with a thump on Meg's back.

Within minutes, everybody was shrieking and laughing and uncontrollably whacking each other with every available pillow.

"Mrs. Hansen will — " *Wham!* went Laura's pillow into Meg's face.

"Will what?" Stevie yelled before sending a second pillow in Meg's direction.

"She'll never recognize this room!" Molly screamed out when she hit her target and toppled over Stevie at last.

"Truce! Truce!" Meg cried, but that didn't stop the zooming pillows.

Pretty soon sweaters, jeans, and sweatshirts as well as pillows were flying through the room and the hallway. Molly's mother called up the stairs to ask what all the thumping was about, and got a teddy bear tossed downstairs for an answer.

Finally, the girls' aching arms and croaky voices made them put down their deadly weapons. They collapsed onto the sleeping bags, which were now in a tangle. Every few minutes someone hiccuped in a little burst of leftover laughter or lifted a pillow in a mock threat. But the girls were too exhausted for any further warfare.

"Ugh, we have to set up all over again," Meg said when she surveyed the pillows, plates, paper hats, teddy bears, and duffel bags in heaps all around the room.

"Do we have to?" Stevie groaned when she heard Meg's cleanup orders.

"We have to," Meg said, but she was too tired to deliver her usual lecture about how any Friends 4-Ever sleepovers had to be just so and no other way.

Even without orders, the girls knew what to do, and the straightening of sleeping bags and smoothing of pillows began all over again. When everything was finally arranged according to regulations, Laura giggled.

"Not another pillow fight, I hope," Meg said to her.

"Never," Laura assured everyone. "I was just

thinking that we don't have anything to do now that Molly's here. I mean, usually we start our sleepovers with reading letters, then writing them. Now we won't have to."

"No offense, guys, but as usual, I'm not in the writing mood," Stevie said. "Let's just eat. Then maybe we can read 'The Big Toe,' " she added in her creepiest Count Dracula voice.

The two hours until midnight passed quickly what with all the sampling of food and tingling of spines. Meg appointed herself Chief Clock-Watcher, and at ten minutes to midnight interrupted Stevie's very scary retelling of "The Dead Man's Brains."

"I call this sleepover to order," Meg said with a laugh and a few taps of the hammer she had thought to bring.

"Oh, Meg, do we have to?" Stevie groaned. "Can't we just do what we want?"

"Sure, if what you want is to tell the same old story we know the ending of already when we could be making important New Year's resolutions."

With this, Molly and Laura sat up with interest, and Stevie knew Meg was going to get her way. "All right, all right. What do we do now, Boss?"

"Simple. Just make a resolution. I already made mine," Meg said proudly.

"Organizing Friends 4-Ever, I'll bet," Stevie muttered.

Now Meg looked very annoyed. "How did you guess?" Before waiting for an answer, Meg made her announcement. "My resolution is to think of new things for us to do when Molly comes home for good." Meg let her resolution sink in, then turned to Laura. "You're next."

Laura bit her lip and scrunched her face in concentration. "My New Year's resolution is not to cry as much when Molly leaves us this time, but write a long letter instead."

Everyone looked at Stevie, wondering what nutty resolution she would have. "My resolution, which I really am going to keep this time, is not to send Molly clippings instead of letters. Promise," she said with a determined expression.

"Oh, no, look!" Meg screamed, pointing to the television.

While the girls were busy saying what they would do in the new year, the new year had arrived! The silver ball had fallen, and the television crowds were hugging and screaming.

The girls scrambled through their things and finally found their noisemakers. When they got downstairs they went out to the front yard where all the grown-ups were out on the lawn banging pots and pans and kissing and hugging each other.

The Friends 4-Ever formed a huddle to keep warm, blew their noisemakers as loud as they could, then screamed, "Happy New Year!" to the sky, the trees, and to each other until their feet were frozen and their voices were gone.

"Happy New Year" was the first thing Molly heard when she opened one eye the next morning and saw her mother standing in the doorway.

"It's ten o'clock," Mrs. Quindlen said after whispering, "Happy New Year." "There are doughnuts and juice downstairs."

In a few minutes, more sleepy eyes opened slowly followed by groans, and stretches, and sounds of disappointment that no one had stayed up all night as planned.

"Wait," Molly said, looking for her stuffed bear. She needed something to cuddle in her arms now that all the fun was over.

"Uh-oh, it's the New Year's grumps," Mr. Quindlen said when he saw how sad and sleepy everyone looked when they plopped down in the kitchen chairs.

Nobody laughed.

"Scotty, could you pass the girls the doughnut basket?" Mrs. Quindlen said.

The basket went around the table, but none of the girls took any. Molly tried a tiny sip of orange juice, but even that didn't help her feel any better. Once again, she had forgotten about the not-fun part of sleepovers, the crabby part.

"I always say these things should be called wakeovers, not sleepovers," Mr. Quindlen couldn't resist saying, the way he often did.

Nobody laughed again.

"Well, I was going to save the surprise 'til later, but you girls look like you need one now," Mr. Quindlen announced.

The word *surprise* had its usual effect. "What surprise, Dad?" Molly had to know.

"Well, I want you to call Grandpa out in Kansas, then you'll find out. Stevie, Meg, and Laura can get on the extensions. Grandpa has something to tell all of you."

Sleepy as the girls were, they sprang from their chairs and went out to get on the phones. Mrs. Quindlen had already dialed the Kansas number and handed the receiver of the kitchen phone to Molly.

"Hello, Happy New Year, Grandpa," Molly said when her grandfather answered.

"Happy New Year to you, Molly Melinda," Grandpa Quindlen said. "I've been missing you, and so has that horse you like to ride. I was over the Pollards' place the other day, and that horse looked mighty low. Hmumph. We must have a bad connection here. There's some static on the line."

"Oh, Grandpa, I forgot. Dad said Stevie, Meg, and Laura should listen in. They're on the other phones."

"Hi, Mr. Quindlen," the girls broke in. "We'll try to be more quiet," Meg said, shushing the other two girls in the background. "By the way, Happy New Year."

"Well, Happy New Year to you girls, too. Things haven't been the same here since you girls went back East last summer. It's too quiet."

Though she loved hearing her grandfather's voice, Molly clutched her bear and wondered when he was going to get to the surprise part. Maybe she was getting her own horse.

"I guess it's going to be even more quiet around here now that Molly isn't coming back."

"What do you mean, Mr. Quindlen?" Meg said in a dry, croaky voice.

"Well, now that you girls are getting Molly back, it's going to be kind of quiet here in Cross

114

Plains. That's what I mean," Grandpa Quindlen explained.

"Grandpa, do you mean we're staying here?" Molly asked, almost afraid to hear the answer.

"Yup. Brian Pollard's got the idea he can run this place as well as you and Scotty, so I told your dad and mom it's time to get back to where you belong, which is home for good."

"Oh, Grandpa!" Molly said, as two tears slid down her face. "Really?"

"Really," Grandpa Quindlen answered. " 'Course, I'll expect you back during the summertime for your usual visit, and you can tell Brian what to do about the store windows and all. It's going to be an awfully long time, Molly Melinda, but I'll figure out how to get along without all the crashing on the stairs and our nice lunches at Annie's. Now I'm going to get off so you can scream your heads off without ruining what little hearing I've got left. I'm going to call you back tonight, so we can talk without all of Rhode Island on the other end," he joked before hanging up.

" 'Bye, Grandpa," Molly said, but she was too stunned to put down the receiver. The phone was her connection to Kansas. Though she was in her real home now, her thoughts were two thousand miles away.

Mrs. Quindlen took the receiver from Molly's hand and set it down on the cradle. "It's okay, honey," she said when she saw Molly's dazed expression. "We'll go back next summer for a good long visit. Now we'll have two real homes."

Before Molly even had time to let that sink in, Stevie, Meg, and Laura burst into the kitchen. "You're home, you're home!" they screamed, hugging her tight.

"I can't believe it," Molly said, reaching for a paper napkin to dry a few tears.

"Well, it's true," Mrs. Quindlen said, dabbing her own tears of joy. "Grandpa Quindlen said he's ready to keep house and run the store again. His doctor says work is the best medicine now. Dad's going to go out when he planned to, to tie things up, and ship our things back. Then he'll drive back with Riggs and start teaching again when the new semester starts."

"And we'll be going out there next summer," Molly explained to her friends between sniffles. "Grandpa needs me at the store, and I want to see everybody again. And, of course, there's Chocolate."

"And licorice and peppermints," Stevie joked, ecstatic that her best friend was home at last.

"You can write Kristy," Laura suggested.

"She'll miss you a lot," Meg added. "I guess we're the lucky ones this time."

"I still can't believe I'm home," Molly said, feeling the warmth of her oldest and best friends. Then a sudden thought stopped the sniffles and tears. "Omigosh, Mom what about Mrs. Hansen? Are we going to live with her in our house?"

"Yeah, what about Mrs. Hansen?" Stevie added, wondering where her nice friend would go now.

"Well, believe it or not, the Fischer house you told her about is available just like you said, but to get it she had to put down the rent for this month. So that's where she's moving," Mrs. Quindlen explained. "She'll stay at her daughter's until next week when the movers come to get her things and bring back ours. It will probably be chaos around here when all this happens, but we'll work it out somehow. I still can't believe it myself."

"Neither can I," Molly said.

"I can," Meg piped up. "It was the Friends 4-Ever Rescue Plan. That's what happened."

"Sure, Meg, and the moon's made of green cheese, too," Stevie interrupted.

But that didn't seem to bother Meg one bit. And even Molly began to believe that the plan they hatched in the orange tent a couple of weeks ago had somehow worked.

"There's only one problem," Meg said.

"What now?" Stevie asked, looking as if she might not actually want an answer.

"What do we do with all our stationery?" Meg asked.

"Maybe we can find new pen pals," Laura said. "Like Kristy!"

"Or we can use the stationery to make paper airplanes," Stevie said, zooming around the kitchen with her arms flapping.

Molly's eyebrows were in their thinking position, raised and close together. She looked up at her friends and gave them a huge smile. "I have an idea, but first you have to go home."

"What is it, Molly? Can't you tell us now?" Meg insisted.

"Nope. Just go home, and you'll find out later," Molly said mysteriously. "I have something important I have to do."

The girls left, but they left grumbling about how stubborn Molly could be.

The second they were out the door, Molly dashed upstairs and grabbed three pieces of stationery. Across the top of each one she printed: *THE SECRET NOTE SOCIETY*. When she was done, she began to write.

THE SECRET NOTE SOCIETY

Dear Stevie,
  Look for notes every day
  Hidden in the tree this way.
  I'll write to you in your tree,
  Now you find a spot to write to me!
            Friends 'til the Fire Flies,

Molly

On the second sheet of paper she wrote a note to Meg.

THE SECRET NOTE SOCIETY
Dear Meg,

Look for notes every day
Hidden in your fence post just this way.
I'll leave my notes in this special place
Then leave me one in a secret space.
               C U When the Dew Drops,

Molly

Molly's fingers hurt from gripping her rainbow pencil so hard and writing so fast, but she still had one more note to go. On the third sheet she wrote a note to Laura.

THE SECRET NOTE SOCIETY
Dear Laura,
    When you look for a sparrow, look for a
        note
    In the log cabin birdhouse you'll find what
        I wrote.
    My old stringy hammock will be the right
        spot

To leave me a note when you write me a
lot.
                    Yours 'til the Jelly Rolls

Molly

Molly folded up all three notes and stuck them
in her jeans pocket.

"I have to go out," she said to her puzzled
parents when she went downstairs.

"Where are you going?" her mother called out.

"What are you doing?" her dad wanted to
know.

"Delivering mail," Molly said. "Important
mail."

Molly ran down the street. When she got to
Stevie's she quickly ran to the big maple tree in
the backyard. Grabbing a branch with one hand,
she pulled herself up to the first notch in the
tree and stuck a note there.

"Happy New Year, everyone!" she called out
to the neighborhood from up in the tree. Then
she eased herself to the ground and ran down
the street.

A new year was starting, and she had deliv-
eries to make and messages to share. "I'm back,

everybody," she called out to the sleepy houses. "This time, I'm *really* back."

What happens when Stevie's big brother starts hanging out with girls — and doesn't have time for Stevie anymore? Read Friends 4-Ever #6, FRIENDS 'TIL THE OCEAN WAVES.